A King Production presents…

Rich or Famous
Part 2

JOY DEJA KING
AND CHRIS BOOKER

This novel is a work of fiction. Any references to real people, events, establishments, or locales are intended only to give the fiction a sense of reality and authenticity. Other names, characters, and incidents occurring in the work are either the product of the author's imagination or are used fictitiously, as those fictionalized events and incidents that involve real persons. Any character that happens to share the name of a person who is an acquaintance of the author, past or present, is purely coincidental and is in no way intended to be an actual account involving that person.

ISBN 13: 978-0986004537
ISBN 10: 0986004537
Cover concept by Joy Deja King
Cover/Inside layout and graphic design by www.MarionDesigns.com
Cover Model: Joy Deja King
Editor: Rosie Valenz

Library of Congress Cataloging-in-Publication Data;
A King Production
Rich or Famous Part 2: a novel/by Joy Deja King and Chris Booker
For complete Library of Congress Copyright info visit;
www.joydejaking.com

A King Production
P.O. Box 912, Collierville, TN 38027

"I keep my enemies close. I give 'em enough rope.
They put themselves in the air.
I just kick the chair."
- Jay Z

This Book is Dedicated To My:

Family, Readers and Supporters.
I LOVE you guys so much. Please believe that!!
— Joy Deja King

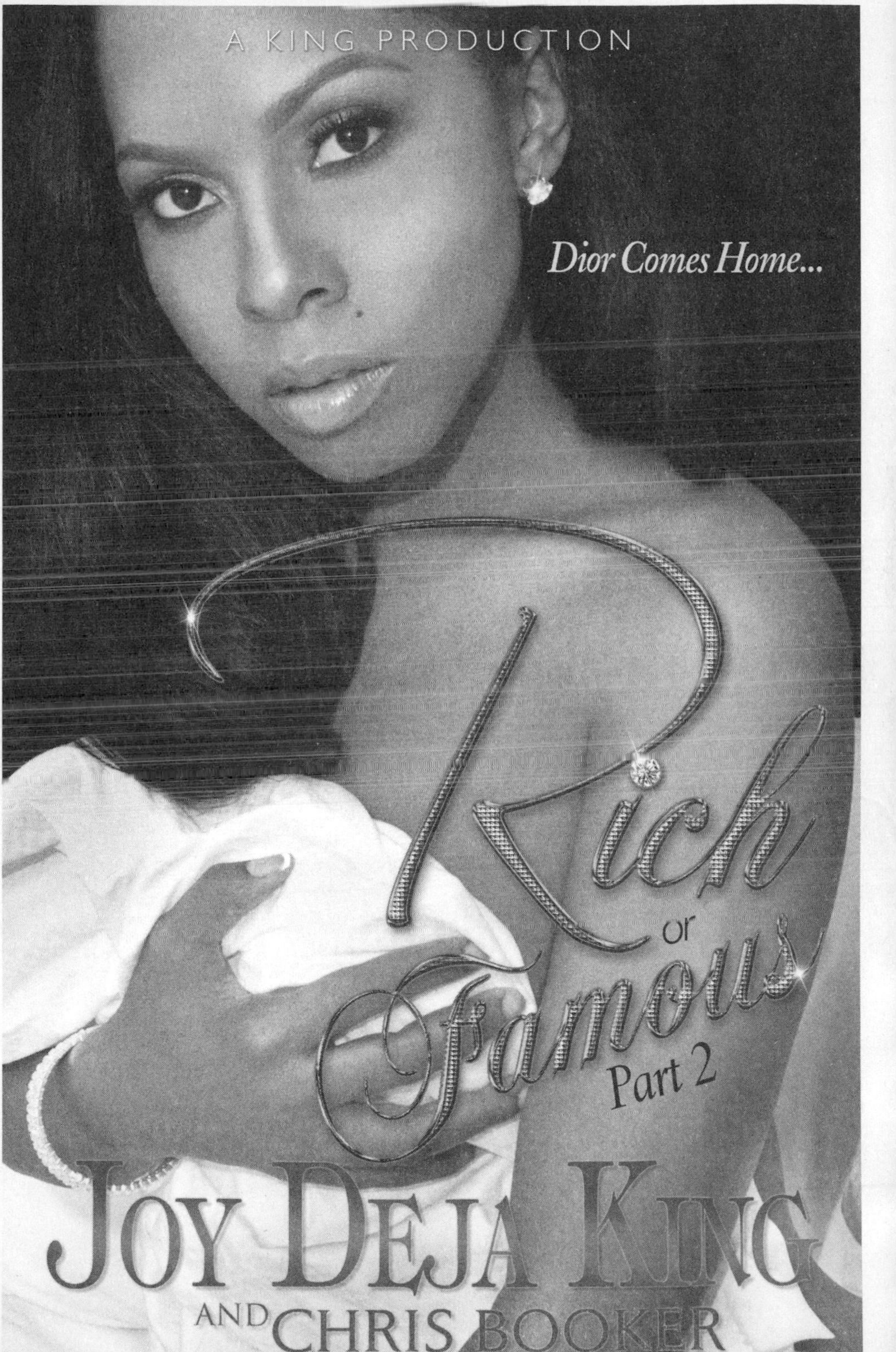
A KING PRODUCTION
Dior Comes Home...
Rich or Famous
Part 2
JOY DEJA KING
AND CHRIS BOOKER

Prologue

Lorenzo

Lorenzo stepped out of his black Bugatti Coupe and entered the non-descript building in East Harlem. Normally, Lorenzo would have at least one henchman with him, but he wanted complete anonymity. When he made his entrance, the man Lorenzo planned on hiring was patiently waiting.

"I hope you came prepared for what I need."

"I wouldn't have wasted my time if I hadn't," Lorenzo stated before pulling out two pictures from a manila envelope and tossing them on the table.

"This is her?"

"Yes, her name is Alexus. Study this face very carefully, 'cause this is the woman you're going to bring to me, so I can kill."

"Are you sure you don't want me to handle it? Murder is included in my fee."

"I know, but personally killing this backstabbing snake is a gift to myself"

"Who is the other woman?"

"Her name is Lala."

"Do you want her dead, too?"

"I haven't decided. For now, just find her whereabouts and any other pertinent information. She also has a young daughter. I want you to find out how the little girl is doing. That will determine whether Lala lives or dies."

"Is there anybody else on your hit list?"

"This is it for now, but that might change at any moment. Now, get on your job, because I want results ASAP," Lorenzo demanded before tossing stacks of money next to the photos.

"I don't think there's a need to count. I'm sure it's all there," the hit man said, picking up one of the stacks and flipping through the bills.

"No doubt, and you can make even more, depending on how quickly I see results."

"I appreciate the extra incentive."

"It's not for you, it's for me. Everyone that is responsible for me losing the love of my life will pay in blood. The sooner the better."

Lorenzo didn't say another word and instead made his exit. He came and delivered; the rest was up to the hit man he had hired. But Lorenzo wasn't worried, he was just one of the many killers on his payroll hired to do the exact same job. He wanted to guarantee that Alexus was delivered to him alive. In his heart, he not only blamed Alexus and Lala for getting him locked up, but also held both of them responsible for Dior taking her own life. As he sat in his jail cell, Lorenzo promised himself that once he got out, if need be he would spend the rest of his life making sure both women received the ultimate retribution.

Chapter 1

Lorenzo walked in a single file line in shackles and handcuffs on his way to the county bus that transported inmates to the courthouse. Today was the hearing to find out if the DA had enough evidence to hold him for trial. This was his second preliminary hearing in two months. The first one was postponed because Lala hadn't shown up. The DA finally got in touch with her and convinced her she would be safe if she came and testified.

The thing about the DA's office is that they lie better than anybody in the courtroom. They told Lala she was going to be safe knowing they didn't give two shits about her or her daughter. All they needed was her testimony, both at the preliminary hearing and at trial.

"Yo son, you know after three times the judge normally throw the case out," Peanut said as he boarded the bus right behind Lorenzo.

Peanut was Lorenzo's celly. They had become cool over the past couple of months finding out that they had a lot in common when it came to the streets and certain family issues. Peanut was locked up for a murder rap. He'd killed a man that had sold his mother some dope, which in turn caused her to overdose. Her death fueled the fire in Peanut to walk up on the man in broad daylight, in front of the entire neighborhood and blow his brains out with a .44 Magnum. He was caught at the scene of the crime sitting right next to the body with the smoking gun in his hand. Lorenzo respected his G. for that and was somewhat envious because he wished he could have found and killed the man who sold his mother the drugs that had her sitting in a mental hospital right now.

"Yeah, well the word is, the snitch is supposed to be in court this time around. My lawyer told me he saw her name on the witness list," Lorenzo said, taking a seat next to the window so he could see some of the city on his way to the courthouse.

"Well, look my dude. Hopefully everything works out for me when I go to get sentenced today. I give you my word, I got you when I touch," Peanut assured him.

Peanut going home would be the break Lorenzo needed. Since he'd been in jail, Lorenzo had cut off a lot of people that were working for him because of how the whole situation had played out with the fake kidnapping and ransom. He could really use some legwork out there, and for many reasons that need not be explained, Lorenzo trusted Peanut.

"I hope everything works out my nigga," Lorenzo said, staring off into the streets. As the bus made its way across town to the courthouse, Lorenzo thought about that last conversation he'd had with Courtney a few months ago. Although it was something he did often, the pain never diminished. Hearing Courtney say that Dior died of a drug overdose always felt like a knife was ripping out his insides. Lorenzo let out a deep sigh and continued staring out the window, trying to push the dismal thoughts out of his mind.

"Ms. Johnson are you ready?" the District Attorney asked Lala when he walked into the small conference room inside the courthouse.

Lala took in a deep breath. "I guess so," she replied nervously.

Lala had to be honest with herself. She really wasn't sure if she wanted to go through with testifying against Lorenzo. The main reason was because she still didn't have all the facts pertaining to the reason why Lorenzo would kill Darell. All she had to go off of was what Alexus had told her, but that alone wasn't sitting right with her. Alexus told her that Lorenzo killed Darell because Darell was stealing money from him. Even if that was the truth, Lala felt there had to be more to the story. Plus, there were never any indications that Darell was stealing, and if anybody had known about it, it would have been her since she dealt with most of Darell's finances.

"Now, I'm going to go over a few things with you before we step into the courtroom," the DA said, taking a seat across the table from Lala.

The DA went over the story Lala had originally told

them from the very beginning. Lala had stated that she overheard Lorenzo telling Darell that he was going to kill him if he found out that he was stealing from him. Lala was adamant that Lorenzo had pulled out an automatic gun on Darell inside of their home and threatened him the same night he was murdered. The whole story was a lie, and the only reason why Lala made it up was because Alexus convinced her to.

Lala had delivered this exact same story in her statements repeatedly, so it was almost impossible for her to take it back now, especially with the pressure of the DA riding her back. Not taking any chances, the detectives on the case escorted her directly to the courthouse. They were determined to bring Lorenzo Taylor down and Lala was the star witness they needed to make it happen.

"Well, what about me and my little girl? Is it going to be safe for us after I testify?" Lala asked, knowing how vicious Lorenzo could be. Even while locked up the streets still had a lot of love and loyalty for him.

"Oh sure, you guys are going to be safe," the DA lied, faking like he cared about Lala and her daughter.

Lala could sense the deceit in his tone. She had a feeling the DA was only saying what he knew she needed to hear, so she would get on that witness stand and testify. The longer the conversation continued, the more on edge Lala became. Lala was well aware that whatever decision she made could possibly put her life and the life of her daughter in grave danger.

Chapter 2

Dior sat on the bench outside of the Rockview Rehabilitation Center in deep thought. The setting seemed more like a luxury getaway, instead of where addicts came who were battling their drug addictions at a place smack in the middle of the National Forest in Buffalo, New York. The lush acres were filled with beautiful gardens, wallabies, lakes and one-of-a-kind trees. The centerpiece was a soothing yet stunning 120-foot waterfall supported by huge rocks, which split into two Mediterranean-style ponds with a curved stream running through it. There was a raised front edge for seating and easy viewing. The landscape gave a mountain feel with large boulders and evergreen trees and a bridge to walk over. It was a stress reliever for many residents who would sit on the benches that lined the pond and escape into serenity.

Dior's daily routine at the center had now become second nature to her. It was a drastic change from when she had first arrived. Months ago she showed up to the treatment center desperate, alone and scared. After Lorenzo got locked up, Dior had quickly turned back to her bad habits. He had become her crutch, and with Lorenzo gone she fell apart. After almost overdosing, Dior finally realized that if she didn't beat her addiction she would end up dead. Leaving her past life behind, especially Lorenzo, was the hardest decision she had ever made. But Dior knew it was the only choice that would save her life.

"What's the matter?" You haven't said two words all day," Erick, Dior's sponsor said as they sat by the tennis courts.

"I apologize. I just have a lot on my mind," Dior replied, brushing some lint off her pants.

"Do you want to talk about it? You know that's what I'm here for," he smiled.

Dior looked at him and smiled back. Erick was a nice guy aside from the fact that he never backed down and was extremely firm. Dior knew it was only because he wanted her to stay on the right track, but it could sometimes be overwhelming. It didn't hurt though that Erick was easy on the eyes. He stood about 6 feet tall, with a strong, athletic build. He kept himself groomed very well and definitely had a grown man swag thing going on.

"So are you going to tell me what you're thinking about?" Erick asked again, since of course he was the type that never backed down.

Initially, Dior hesitated to answer Erick truthfully. But she knew part of her process to recovery was being able to openly discuss the painful things in her life.

"I was thinking about this man I was deeply in love with. I really don't even know why I left him the way that I did. He was nothing but good to me even though I found out he had cheated," Dior admitted, looking down at her hands as she rubbed her fingers together nervously. She seemed to be doing that more and more. But it was either that or pick her smoking habit back up. Dior figured rubbing her fingers together had a lot less health risk than cigarettes.

"See, that's where I have to stop you," Erick interrupted. "You have to stop your old ways of thinking. A good man would never cheat on his significant other."

"I guess you're right," Dior agreed, nodding her head. "But people do make mistakes. I mean obviously I've made a ton of them."

"I understand that and I don't knock the next man on how he do his thing. But when it comes to the people I care about, I'ma keep it real," Erick said. "But go ahead and finish. I didn't mean to cut you off."

"After all this time, I still miss him like crazy. But I know he might spend the rest of his life in jail. Hell, even if he got out, I don't think he would still want to be with me after all the lies," Dior said softly. "I turned my back on him when he needed me the most. He's sitting in jail and I'm out here..." Dior paused.

"You're sitting out here trying to get your own life together," Erick reminded her. "Before you can help anybody else, you have to help yourself."

"You have all the answers don't you?" Dior smiled.

"Nah, just the ones that make sense," he shot back.

Dior looked up at him and continued to smile. She really did appreciate having Erick in her life. Dior felt at ease with him. He was the type of person she could discuss just about anything with. And she knew he would always be honest with her no matter what.

"I also..." Dior began, but caught herself.

"What?" Erick inquired, seeing that she was hesitant. "Don't hold back. I'm here to help you deal with all of your problems," he said.

"I know everything you're saying is probably right, but I want him back."

"Dior, you don't want to replace one addiction with another."

"What do you mean?"

"You've been clean for some time now. Are you trying to run back to this man, even though he might not be good for you, so you can focus on something else besides drugs? Chasing love isn't going to stop your battle with addiction."

"I get that, but…" Dior's voice trailed off as she tried to make sense of her thoughts.

"Listen, I understand your struggle. I battled my own addiction, and it was to sex."

"Really?"

"Yes. But I'm winning. Can you believe I've been celibate for almost a year?" Erick said with pride.

"Get the hell out of here! And I had the nerve to be feeling some type of way about my dry spell," Dior laughed.

Dior found it fascinating that a man so handsome and who clearly had his choice of women, had opted to be sex-free. That decision made her respect him even more and feel lucky that he was her sponsor.

"I made the choice of celibacy because I was tired of sleeping around with different women almost every night. I made a vow to myself that I wouldn't have sex until the right woman came into my life. The choice wasn't easy but once I made it, I stuck to it and my life has been better ever since."

"I admire your self-control," Dior admitted.

"That's what this program is helping you learn, Dior. Life is about choices. Making the right ones and sticking to it."

"So you're saying going back to the man I'm in love with isn't the right choice for me?""

"Only you know the answer to that. But just remember, there is a reason why you left him in the first place. And with that, our session is up," Erick said, looking down at his watch..

"Ahhh, things were just getting good," Dior said, rolling her eyes and chuckling at the same time.

"I know, but we'll have to continue this in our next session. I have a meeting with the administration in about five minutes. I give you my word, we'll pick things right back up tomorrow," Erick said, getting up from his chair.

Dior smiled as Erick walked across the tennis courts. She was finally making a breakthrough by sharing some of her feelings regarding Lorenzo. She had kept those emotions so guarded, but Dior knew in order for

Erick to truly help her, she couldn't hold anything back. For the first time since she had been at Rockview, things were starting to get interesting.

A knock at the front door woke Lala out of her sleep. She looked over and saw that the knocks hadn't woken up Tania.

"Who da fuck is this knocking on my shit this late at night?" Lala mumbled to herself as she got out of the bed and grabbed the .38 from her dresser.

She eased down the steps with caution with the gun down by her side. Even though Lala hadn't testified at Lorenzo's hearing, she was still a little bit on the paranoid side. The hearing was only postponed for a week because right before she was about to take the stand, Lala came down with severe stomach cramps. To make her lie more believable, she fell out in the hallway right before she entered the courtroom. Lala even had them call an ambulance to take her to the emergency room. At the time, that seemed like a better option than having to come face-to-face with Lorenzo. But Lala knew her theatrics wouldn't work a second time and she was trying to come up with a plan to get out of this mess she was knee deep in. She didn't know if Lorenzo was going to send somebody to shut her up permanently, so Lala was pretty much stashed up in the house all day and night.

Before Lala answered the door, she walked over to the window and pulled back the curtains slightly. At first she couldn't see anybody, but then Alexus came out of the shadows, banging on the door again. Lala walked over to the door, tucking the .38 in her back pocket. She slung the door open right before Alexus was about to bang on it again.

"Damn, Alexus! What's going on?" Lala spit with an attitude.

Lala didn't even notice the man standing off to the side. Without even asking, Alexus and the man that was with her entered the house. Lala let them pass but immediately grabbed ahold of the butt of the .38.

"Yo, what happened to you testifying the other day at Lorenzo's hearing?" Alexus asked, flopping down on the couch. "I hope you not gettin' cold feet on me."

"On you?" Lala asked, slamming the front door behind her. "I'm not doing it for you. I'm doing it because that nigga killed my baby father...right?" she asked with an attitude.

During the whole conversation Alexus noticed that Lala never brought her hand from behind her back, nor did she move from her position by the door. The guy Alexus brought with her also noticed the same thing and it didn't take a genius to figure out she was strapped.

"Yeah, that's right. Word is, Lorenzo killed him because he wouldn't give up all the money he stole from him and the rest of the people your kid's father robbed blind," Alexus snapped back, looking around the room in a suspicious manner.

"What do you mean money he stole? My baby father didn't steal from nobody," Lala shot back.

"You really don't know what's going on, do you?" Alexus said to Lala as she looked over at the man standing over by the television. "Your baby father supposed to have a few million stashed away somewhere and right before Lorenzo put a bullet in his head he told me about it," Alexus explained.

Lala knew Alexus was up to something from the moment she walked into the house, she just didn't know what it was until now. If that was true and Darnell did leave behind millions of dollars, Lala was unaware of where it was. He had never told her about any money other than the 135k he had left in their safe.

"So that's what this is about?" Lala questioned. "You here because you think I know where the money is at? Even if I did know, what makes you think I would tell you where it was?"

Alexus gave a fake smile then stood up from the couch. "You see my friend Brice standing over there?" Alexus asked, nodding in his direction. "If you don't find that money and hand it over to me, he's gonna see to it that you meet Darell on the other side," Alexus threatened.

On hearing that Lala pulled the .38 from her back pocket and pointed it at Alexus. Brice reacted by drawing his weapon and pointing it at Lala. The threat on her life really had Lala on the brink of destruction. Alexus on the other hand couldn't care less. She really didn't have much to lose at this point. The million dollars she and Brice had scammed Lorenzo out of was just about gone already. Aside from the few thousand dollars she had on her, Alexus was broke. On top of that, she had picked up a bad cocaine habit that had her spending money hourly.

"Nah, Brice, we ain't gone do it like this," Alexus said, waving for him to lower his gun, which he did cautiously. "Look Lala, I'm not tryna take it there with you because of Darell's mistakes. I just need the money he left behind and I need you to make sure Lorenzo never come home again. 'Cause if he do get out he's not gonna hesitate to have both of us killed," Alexus said, only reiterating what Lala already knew.

Lala watched Alexus walk towards the door. She debated on whether or not to pull the trigger and blow Alexus' head off before she left the house. But she decided against it, thinking about Tania, who was upstairs asleep.

"Find the money so we can split it and get da hell out of here before shit get ugly," Alexus said, as she along with Brice, finally made their exit.

Chapter 3

"Don't you get caught up with that boy. He's a regular Casanova," Ms. Ferra told Dior as they were power walking on the trail behind the facility.

"What?" Dior smiled. "I'm not getting caught up with anybody," she said, knowing exactly who Ms. Ferra was talking about.

"Girl, don't lie to me. I see the way the two of you make those goo-goo eyes at each other," Ms. Ferra laughed as she slowed down her pace.

Ms. Ferra was probably the only friend Dior accepted while being in rehab. She was much older and wiser than Dior but had a youthful vibe with her. She was also somewhat of an actress, that is, when she wasn't spending time in rehab for abusing alcohol. A judge sentenced her to three months in rehab for multiple DUIs, a hit and run and disorderly conduct. She was so well-known by the State Troopers that they nicknamed her Freeway Ferra.

"Ms. Ferra, I don't have time to be messing around with Erick. It ain't shit he could do for me and better yet, it ain't shit I can do for him right now," Dior said stopping to take a swig from her water bottle.

Dior had to admit there was something she found intriguing about Erick, and on occasion there had been some flirting. But Dior knew it wasn't a smart move to even consider crossing the line with her sponsor. Plus, Dior's heart still belonged to Lorenzo. She thought about him all day, every day, seven days out of the week. If anything, Erick was only a distraction because she was spending so much time with him and he had become a confidante.

"Ms. Ferra can I ask you something?" Dior said in a serious tone. "Have you ever loved somebody so much that it made you question whether or not that person loved you back the same?" Dior wanted to know.

Ms. Ferra chuckled at the question coming from a woman that was young enough to be her child. "Little girl, I'll be 55 next week," she said looking down at the date on her watch. "I been in love so many times I think I slipped up and gave Cupid some pussy before," she joked. Dior couldn't help but laugh at how unfiltered Ms. Ferra could be with some of her comments.

Now, if you're asking me if I thought any of the men I loved loved me back, then my answer to you is yes," Ms. Ferra continued. "Out of all the men I been with, I truly believe that only one ever loved me the same, if not more then I loved him," she smiled gazing out into the horizon.

"You better not be talking about Mr. Tucker, the swimming instructor," Dior joked, tapping Ms. Ferra on her hip.

"Nah baby, I'm talking about Matthew, my current husband. This man loves me so much...Wait, let me just show you," Ms. Ferra said, reaching into her waist pouch and pulling out a small cell phone. "Now you better not tell anybody I got this," she said looking around to make sure other residents from the facility weren't around.

Dior looked around too, because having a cell phone was a violation in the program and every violation was an infraction. If any resident got more than five infractions in the program they would be kicked out and wouldn't be able to reapply for six months. Ms. Ferra had three infractions already.

"Hey honey, what you doing?" Ms. Ferra spoke into the phone.

She put the phone on speaker so that Dior could hear the conversation. Ms. Ferra began asking her husband a number of questions pertaining to the time and place they met, what clothes she'd had on and how her hair was done. She asked him about things they did during their marriage like places they'd gone and things they'd seen. Then she asked him about personal things pertaining to her body, which he knew every inch of, including a small mole the size of a small dot that rested under her right breast. He had an answer for every question she asked, which was very impressive.

"Do you love me, Matthew?" was Ms. Ferra's final question.

"You know Ferra, out of all the questions you just asked me, that was the dumbest of them all. Of course I love you Fe Fe. So hurry up and come back home to me 'cause I need you here, by my side," Matthew said, in a sincere tone.

"I love you too, Matt," Ms. Ferra responded before she hung up the phone.

The conversation she'd just heard made Dior want to snatch the phone and call Lorenzo, just to hear his voice. The only thing that stopped her was the fact that she'd promised herself that this stint in the rehab was her opportunity to start fresh. She didn't want to relive the past. In order for her to get better, Dior felt she had to focus on the future.

A light knock at the door got Dior to turn from looking out of the window.

"Come in," she yelled, then turned to finish looking outside.

"You know, when this place was built, the architect wanted every window to have a breathtaking view," Erick said as he entered Dior's room.

"I'm sure you're going to tell me the reason behind that," she smiled, taking a sip of the hot tea in her mug.

"Actually, that view is a significant part of your recovery," Erick said, walking up beside her and looking out of the window.

"It gives you a sense of peace and tranquility. At times when your body seems tense, the view can be relaxing. Hell, mountains with snow covering the top of them in the summer time is something most city people hardly ever see," he said, taking in the view himself. "For people like us, it's like being introduced to something precious for the first time," he spoke softly, then turned to look at Dior.

Even if he tried, Erick couldn't ignore how beautiful Dior was. As the sun beamed off the side of her face her beauty intensified. Detoxing from the drugs and alcohol really brought out her true skin complexion and added moisture, which made her skin shine naturally. Her hair grew thicker, longer and her face became fuller due to the few pounds she had picked up. She also gained some weight in a few other places, making her body more voluptuous. Dior's vibrant natural beauty definitely had her looking much better than before.

"What are you looking at?" Dior asked, feeling his eyes all over her. "And what do I owe the pleasure of you coming to visit me?" she playfully asked, trying to break his stare.

"Oh yeah," he said, snapping out of his daze. "I came to tell you how proud I am of you for all the progress you're making."

"Thank you, but you deserve a lot of the credit."

"But you've put in the necessary work. So much so that the administration feels you're getting closer to getting a definitive release date."

"A release…wow, do you think I'm ready for that?"

"Dior, don't panic. We're not putting you out tomorrow," Erick smiled.

"Does this have something to do with me having no money?"

"I told you, I've already taken care of that. Whatever the cost of your treatment, I have it covered. You can stay at Rockview for however long you want, but I personally believe you'll be ready to go back home soon. But it's up to you."

"Thank you so much Erick," she said, leaning in to hug him.

Dior was grateful for everything Erick had done for her up to this point. When she came to the Rockview facility she was only able to pay for a couple of weeks' worth of treatment. Right when she was about to be discharged due to her lack of funds, Erick came out of nowhere and paid for her to stay another week. That week led to him paying for another week, then another week until he finally said, "Fuck it," and paid for her full stay, which had cost him a pretty penny. Dior didn't know his reasons for doing it, but it had to come from a positive place. He actually had become keen to seeing Dior's success with the program.

Erick had watched as an ill-mannered, cocaine snorting, alcoholic junkie changed her ways with every day that passed. Dior was one of the few residents who had multiple addictions to focus on. Based on the history at the treatment facility, Dior's kind always failed. But she was proving to be the exception, which impressed Erick. That's the reason he didn't mind coming out of his pocket to pay for her treatment. Dior had become his little project and he couldn't wait to see what she would blossom into.

Chapter 4

Lorenzo's court hearing was only two days away and all he could concentrate on was the warning the Judge had given the DA at his last appearance. He had made it clear that if they didn't present their homicide witness, those charges would be dismissed from the indictment. If that was to happen, Lorenzo's lawyers were going to shoot for bail with the remaining drug charges. The homicide charge was the only thing that was preventing him from getting out in the first place. The rest of their case was rather weak. Lorenzo was itching to get back out on the streets so that he could take care of some unfinished business. Alexus was at the top of his list, along with whoever helped her pull off that million-dollar scam. Second, he had to find out who was the rat in his circle that got him stuck with numerous drug charges. The DA had hinted around a couple possible names during one of the hearings, but couldn't get any further into the details because of the homicide being at the forefront of the case.

"Taylor, you got a visitor," the correctional officer announced, tapping on his cell door while doing the morning count.

Lorenzo looked at his celly with a strange look on his face. He wasn't expecting any visitors this weekend due to Phenomenon's busy schedule with club appearances for his new single that had just dropped a couple days ago. It wasn't a legal visit because the guard would have told him to bring his paperwork.

"Damn son. Somebody must love da kid," Peanut said, looking up at the TV.

"I wasn't expecting nobody. And you know how much a nigga don't like pop-up visits," Lorenzo responded. When he got to the visiting room and gave the guard his I.D. he looked around the crowded room for a familiar face. At first he didn't see anybody he recognized, but as he walked further into the room he heard someone yelling out his name.

"Uncle Lorenzo," a little voice yelled from the crowd of visitors. When he looked to see who it was, Tania was running towards him with a huge smile on her face and her arms wide open. He reached down and scooped her up off the ground, giving her a big hug.

I know dis bitch ain't bold enough to come up here after she was the reason why I'm in here in the first place, Lorenzo thought to himself as he walked through the visiting room. When he got to the section Tania led him to, Lala was sitting there looking back at Lorenzo shaking her head. She really didn't know what to expect from Lorenzo, but she was certain her face was the last he wanted to see. Lala was one of the main reasons he was locked up, but that was the main reason she'd brought Tania along. She knew how much Lorenzo loved her and as long as Tania was around, he wasn't going to touch Lala.

"Mommy look," Tania said, pointing at Lorenzo.

"Yeah baby, I see him," Lala replied, giving a fake smile.

"I always knew you was crazy," Lorenzo said, taking a seat across from her. "What you doin' here, Lala?" Lorenzo asked, as he tickled Tania so she wouldn't pay attention to what he was saying.

"Tania wanted to see you. She kept asking about you so I told her I would bring her to come see you," Lala explained.

"Did you tell her you was about to kill me," he said in a sarcastic but serious way, all the while still making Tania laugh.

"No, I didn't tell her that, nor did I tell her that you was the one who killed her dad," she countered, in a low tone so Tania wouldn't hear her.

"I didn't kill Darell," he barked back a little too loud. He looked down at Tania lying on his lap and started tickling her again, hoping she didn't hear or understand what he had said. She just laughed it off, not knowing anything but how happy she was to see Lorenzo. "Tania, have you been a good girl?" he asked, sitting her up on his lap.

"Yes Uncle Lorenzo. I'm good sometimes," she answered in the cutest, most innocent voice.

"Sometimes?" he asked, smiling and tickling her neck. "You gotta be a good girl all the time."

"I'm not going to go through with it," Lala spoke. "They want me back in court on Monday but I'm not going to show," she said, reaching over and fixing Tania's shirt.

"Yeah, I'll believe it when I see it. That snake Alexus got you fucked up in the head," he stated.

"Ooooooohhh! Uncle Lorenzo said a bad word," Tania giggled, pointing up at Lorenzo's face. Lorenzo patted his lips as a punishment then let Tania do the same thing. Lala just looked on. He was so good with Tania. That little girl loved him just about as much as she loved her own dad. That was just another one of the many reasons she couldn't go through with testifying against him.

"Alexus came by the house last night. She had some guy with her and she was talking crazy."

"Wait, Alexus is back in the city?" Lorenzo asked, as her name snapped him out of playing mode. "Last thing I heard, her and Brice went out to Cali."

"Nah, she's back and she talking about some money that Darell left behind. She got a crazy idea that I know where it is."

"Well do you?" Lorenzo stared directly in Lala's eyes waiting for her response.

"No, I swear I don't know what she's talking about."

From experience Lorenzo knew that if Alexus was inquiring about some money, then nine times out of ten she knew something. That wasn't gonna be good for Lala or Tania because it was already proven that Alexus would do anything for the money. She didn't care whose life she had to take in order to get it.

Chapter 5

Dior was excited because Erick had told her that he had something special planned for her today. He had given her instructions to be dressed and waiting at the main building in twenty minutes. Dior didn't know what that surprise was but she hauled ass and got in the shower. She was dressed within fifteen minutes and on her way out the door. She kept it basic with a pair of jeans, a white tank top and a pair of classic red pumps. Her hair was pulled back into a ponytail and covering her lips was Mac Russian Red lipstick.

On her way to the main building Dior decided to stop by and check up on Ms. Ferra, who's apartment was two floors below her. When she walked up to the door, Dior could hear the sounds of Marvin Gaye singing *I Want You*. Ms. Ferra always loved listening to her oldies. Dior knocked on the door but Ms. Ferra didn't answer. She waited then knocked on the door again. This time Dior could hear Ms. Ferra singing in the background.

Out of curiosity, Dior checked the door knob and was somewhat shocked that the door was open.

"Ms. Ferra!" Dior called out, slowly entering her room. "Oh shit, Ms. Ferra!" Dior belted, seeing her halfway passed out on the couch with a bottle of Brandy dangling from her hand. "Ms. Ferra, what are you doing?" Dior said, taking the bottle out of her hand. Dior walked to the kitchen and poured what was left of the Brandy into the sink.

Ms. Ferra kept singing to the music, slurred words and all. She was pissy drunk. Dior knew that if she was caught like this it was an automatic termination. Ms. Ferra would be escorted off the premises before the day was over.

"Come on, I gotta get you in the bed," Dior said, leaning down and wrapping Ms. Ferra's arm around her neck. "What was you thinking?" she said with concern as she helped her to her feet.

Ms. Ferra started laughing and trying to talk at the same time. "I was thinking about getting fuuuucked up tonight," she chuckled as Dior led her back to her room. "You know, Dior, I got a problem. I drink too much," she laughed, falling face first onto her bed.

There was no way Dior was going to go anywhere with Erick and leave Ms. Ferra here like this. Dior considered Ms. Ferra to be a friend and there was no way she was leaving her in this condition.

"Now, Ms. Ferra, I need you to stay right here until I get back," Dior said, as she took off her shoes.

"Are you mad at me, Dior?" Ms. Ferra whined, changing

her laughter in a cry. "Please don't be mad at me," she pleaded.

"I'm not mad at you. I just need to take care of something real quick," Dior explained.

"You gone tell on me? Please don't tell on me.... cause you know snitches get stitches," Ms. Ferra joked, laughing at her own self. Dior had to chuckle at the comment.

"I promise I'm not gonna tell on you. Just stay here until I get back," Dior said, leaving the room and closing Ms. Ferra's bedroom door behind her. She needed to call Erick to cancel for tonight but didn't want to take any chances of him hearing Ms. Ferra's drunken voice in the background. Although Dior would never tell on her, Erick was an employee and he was obligated to report any residents breaking the rules. So Dior wasn't taking any chances.

When Ms. Ferra woke up her head was spinning. She hadn't felt like this in a while, considering for the last two months she had been completely sober. She sat up on the bed then looked around her room only to see Dior sitting in a chair asleep.

"Oh God," she mumbled to herself, lowering her head into her cupped hands. The shameful feeling of relapsing kicked in and the thought of having to start all over again immediately weighed down heavy on her.

"Look who's up," Dior said, stretching and yawning in the chair. "I got you some Alka Seltzer in the kitchen,"

Dior said, getting up. Ms. Ferra got up and followed her to the kitchen.

"I'm sorry you had to see me like that. I was..."

"You don't owe me any apologies," Dior said, cutting her off. "I haven't seen one person in this program who is perfect. We make mistakes. We fall and then we pick ourselves up and try again. All you can do is move forward now."

"Wow. Hearing that come from you means a lot," Ms. Ferra said, taking a seat at the kitchen table. "I know one thing though, my head is spinning like a tornado," she said placing her two fingers against her temple.

"Here drink this," Dior instructed, placing a cup on the table in front of her. "Now, we have group session in a hour so you gotta down this and hop in the shower."

Ms. Ferra couldn't believe how much concern and support Dior was showing her. Normally, when Ms. Ferra has fallen off the wagon, everybody except her husband Matthew turned their back on her. "Why are you doing all this?" Ms. Ferra asked, looking down at the concoction Dior had put together.

Dior walked over from the sink and took a seat at the table with Ms. Ferra. She would be lying if she said that going out with Erick wasn't that important to her because she really was looking forward to getting off the grounds for a few hours. But Dior honestly felt like she was obligated as a friend to put aside her own personal wants in order to help Ms. Ferra. It was a big step for Dior, being as though she spent her entire adult life being selfish and self-centered, wanting the world to revolve around her.

"I'm your friend, Ms. Ferra. And what kind of friend would I be if I left you here, knowing you were in trouble?" Dior reasoned, pushing the cup into Ms. Ferra's hand.

"You really did that because you're my friend?" Ms. Ferra asked, looking up at Dior with tears beginning to fill her eyes.

Dior smiled. "I would call you my sister but you're old enough to be my mother," she laughed. "Besides, if I would have left you in here like that you was bound to get into something and I couldn't let that happen," Dior said, rubbing Ms. Ferra's shoulder.

"Girl, you have a good point. Right before you came I was about to go up to the administrators office, pull my pants down and tell him to kiss my ass," Ms. Ferra clowned, taking a large gulp of the concoction.

They both sat there and laughed at the thought of it. Dior and Ms. Ferra were always cool and had grown closer over the last few weeks, but today they had reached a momentous point in their relationship. They had cemented their bond as friends, without even having to say it. The two of them were going to ride this program out together, no matter what obstacles were ahead of them.

Chapter 6

"You think she knows where that money is?" Brice asked Alexus, walking into the kitchen where she was sitting.

"If she don't know where it is, I'm sure she's gonna be looking for it," Alexus answered, as she straightened out two lines of cocaine on the glass table.

She took the rolled up 20 dollar bill, put it in her nose, leaned down and sniffed one of the lines. She threw her head back and covered her nose with her finger as if she was preventing any residue or drippage from falling back out. Alexus sat there frozen for a minute, letting the cocaine set in.

Brice looked on, not really that big on snorting anything up his nose. He was just waiting on the benefit of being around Alexus when she got high. It didn't take long for Alexus to start feeling it. She got up from the kitchen table after snorting another line, walked over to the stereo system and turned some music on.

She slowly danced her way back over to Brice

with a seductive look in her eyes. He sat back in the chair with a smile on his face, knowing she was ready. She immediately straddled him on the chair, grabbed a handful of his cheeks and began kissing him. She stuffed her tongue deep down his throat as his hands caressed her ass. She jumped up, took two steps back and began lifting her shirt over her head. Brice reached over and unbuttoned her pants, then took off his shirt. Alexus grabbed his hand and led him over to the couch where she pushed him down onto it. It took seconds for her to undue his pants, reach in and pull out his dick.

"Who got the best head in the world?" Alexus asked, looking up at him while slowly kissing the head of his dick.

"Dat be you, ma," Brice answered.

In the mist of kissing it, Alexus took his massive tool into her mouth, making it disappear in one gulp. Her warm, wet throat felt like virgin pussy the way it collapsed around every inch of it. Brice leaned his head back in pleasure as Alexus began to slowly bob her head up and down, pushing his dick deep into her throat.

"Damn, girl," Brice moaned, placing his right hand on the back of her head as a means to guide her.

He looked down at her, watching how her full, thick, soft lips caressed his manhood every time she came up and went back down on it. Brice could feel himself about to cum, and right before he did Alexus pulled up off of him. It was like she could feel it coming on.

"Scoot up some," Alexus told him so that his ass was at the edge of the couch.

Alexus stood up and pulled her panties off. There was no need for Brice to return the favor of giving Alexus some head because her pussy got wet just from sucking his dick. Besides, at that point all she wanted to do was feel him inside of her. She turned around and straddled him backwards, grabbing the base of his dick and guiding it into her insides until she was able to sit down on it completely.

She grinded back and forth for a minute then leaned forward all the way until her hands were on the floor. She began bouncing her ass up and down on his dick at a steady pace, all the while looking back at it. Brice knew he couldn't take much more of this. He reached up, palmed both of her ass cheeks and began bouncing her ass harder onto his dick. A clear vision of his dick sliding in and out of her brought him to squeeze off. His cum shot up in her, and the more his warm fluids filled her up, the more she began to reach her climax.

"Oooooh shiiiit!," Alexus whined, speeding up the pace as she reached her climax.

Alexus fell back onto Brice's chest exhausted. He knew that his work was done and he had pleased her sexual appetite once again. That was, until Alexus started grinding her hips back and forth slowly, indicating to Brice that round two was underway.

★★★★★

The visit from Lala the other day messed Lorenzo's head up something crazy. He really didn't know what to think about most of the things they had discussed, but there were two things he was certain about. He didn't trust Lala. She was only interested in protecting her own ass and she had no problem using her daughter to try and soften his disgust for her. He also knew that Alexus was devious and manipulative and that she needed to be put down once and for all. Lorenzo held both of them responsible for being locked up but also for losing Dior, especially Lala. Lorenzo believed it was the fact that Lala had told Dior about that night they'd had sex and had embellished the status of their relationship that sent Dior over the edge and led to her drug overdose. Dealing with both of those women would be Lorenzo's top priority whenever he got out from behind these bars.

"Hey, pack your stuff. R&D just called for you," the correctional officer yelled out through the cell door.

Peanut jumped up from doing push-ups and walked over to the door. Lorenzo, who was lying in his bunk reading, peeked over the book to see what was going on.

"What am I going to R&D for?" Peanut asked the guard, as he was getting ready to walk off.

"You're outta here, I'm guessing," the guard answered before walking away. Peanut turned to look at Lorenzo, who had a smile on his face.

"Nigga, you goin' home," Lorenzo grinned, tossing the book to the side.

Last time Peanut went to court he had signed a deal for six years in order to plead guilty to 3rd degree murder. His time had been served because he'd already been locked up for four years waiting to go to trial, and in the state of New York you only do four years off a six year bid. Even though Peanut had that time in, he still had a detainer lodged against him. That meant he couldn't be released until he got the opportunity to see his old judge about an open drug case that he caught right before he got locked up for the murder. That's the reason Peanut was confused about being called to R&D. There were only three things R&D was mainly used for: If you were just getting locked up, if you were on your way up North to the penitentiary, or if you were being released to go home.

"Yo, my nigga. I don't know what's going on but you got all of my info. Whenever these crackers let me out, I got you son," Peanut said as he rounded up his pictures and legal work.

Lorenzo hoped Peanut was getting released back out into the world. He definitely could use somebody on the streets to do some footwork. Most of the key people Lorenzo did have out there were missing in action. A lot of business needed to be dealt with and as the cell door closed, Lorenzo was counting on Peanut to be that man.

*****

"So how was the group session?" Erick asked as Dior made her way over to the outside picnic tables where he was sitting.

"It was cool," she answered sitting down at the table. "I know one thing. I can't wait to get out of here."

"Why, what you in a rush for?" Eric asked, turning to face her. "I mean, what do you have planned for your first month or so back in the city? You know how ugly it can get out there." Erick never painted any fairytale stories.

There was no denying that when you entered the cold and often cruel world of New York City you always needed to keep one eye open or risk becoming just another lost soul. But they say there's no place like NYC, and the allure always kept its victims coming back for more.

"I wanna get back into the industry. But this time minus all the drugs and alcohol," Dior declared with confidence.

"Oh yeah, I meant to tell you that I saw you in the Guy Phenomenon video. You looked hot," he smiled. "I bet you miss that life."

"Yeah, I do. I was on my way to having it all… being rich and famous." Dior started to go on about her previous life and all the great things that came along with it.

Erick busted out laughing. He couldn't help himself listening to Dior go on about what she considered to be "living it up."

"What's so funny?" Dior smiled, punching Erick in his arm.

"Nothin' man. You just talk like you was doin' somethin' out there. It's just funny, that's all."

"I was doin' somethin'," Dior snapped, becoming a tad defensive.

"Whoa, whoa, whoa, don't get mad at me. You the one who said you had it all," Erick said as he continued to chuckle.

"Actually I said I was on my way to having it all, and I was. You think I'm lying," Dior shot back.

She was starting to take it personally, but that's exactly what Erick wanted her to do. He knew that somewhere deep down inside Dior was still on her little high horse.

"Nah ma. I don't think you're lying. I just think you have the wrong idea of what 'having it all' means. For instance, you were dealing with Sway Stone. He had what many consider money and fame, but he wasn't smart at all."

"Oh now you checking up on who I was messing with. Is that a part of being a sponsor too?" Dior cracked.

"Dior, your relationship with him was all over the blogs, the internet and magazines. I didn't have to check up on you because your business was already out there. Now, if you want me to keep it real with you like a friend, I can do that, but if you want me to be your sponsor then I can do that too. I just thought we was better than that," Erick said, now becoming serious himself.

At this point Dior had an attitude and she really didn't feel like talking anymore. She didn't know whether it was the way Erick questioned her fame in the industry or the fact that he knew so much about her personal life. Whatever it was, he had rubbed her the wrong way, and at the moment, Dior wanted no part of it.

"Where are you going, Dior?" Eric yelled out as

she walked away. “Come back,” he shouted but Dior kept it moving.

Besides working on her drug and alcohol addictions, Dior was also trying to get her temper under control too. In the past she’d had a tendency of losing it when things weren’t going her way. So instead of exploding, Dior felt the best thing she could do was walk away and finish her conversation with Erick once she got her emotions in check.

Chapter 7

"What da hell is she talking about?" Lala mumbled to herself, pulling out all of her dresser drawers. "Come on, Darell," she continued, going over and pulling out each of Darell's drawers.

Lala searched her house from top to bottom trying to find the millions of dollars Alexus said that Darell had left behind. She didn't know if it was true, but she wasn't about to be sitting on a lost treasure without looking for it. Lala wasn't broke but there was a lot she could do with a couple of million dollars, and at the top of her agenda was to move as far away as possible. Lala was over living in New York, and the only reason she chose to stay after Darell's death was because she actually thought that her and Lorenzo would have a chance to be together. It seemed crazy but she was in love with him and had been since the first time they were intimate. It seemed wrong because he and Darell had been friends, but at the same time it seemed right because Lorenzo knew her so well.

"Mommy, I'm hungry," Tania whined, walking into the room with her pajamas on and her fuzzy bunny slippers. Lala was so busy searching all morning she had forgotten to make breakfast. She felt kind of bad too, because Tania hardly ever had to tell Lala she was hungry.

"Awwwwwwe! Mommy's coming right now. What does my little mini me want to fill her belly up with?" Lala playfully laughed as she picked Tania up and carried her downstairs on her hip.

Once in the kitchen Lala decided that she was going to make a full breakfast, complete with eggs, sausage and blueberry pancakes, Tania's favorite. She wanted to make up for neglecting her daughter all morning. Lala reached up into the kitchen cabinets to get the frying pans and the mixer. This was the first big breakfast she had cooked since she'd been back in the old house, so she was kind of rusty when it came to remembering where everything was. She moved around a few pots and pans until she found the right one, then she searched for the mixer.

"Where are you?" she yelled in annoyance, as she looked around for the mixer. She walked over to the other cabinets, felt on top of the refrigerator and reached all the way in the back.

"What da hell is this," she mumbled to herself, tugging away at a latch that was up against the back wall.

She pulled it but it wouldn't move. That prompted Lala to open up the rest of the cabinet doors that were attached to it. She cleaned the whole cabinet out, placing everything on the table. It was then that Lala noticed another latch in the middle of the cabinet. Reaching in and grabbing both latches, she pulled on them simultaneously. The entire back wall of the cabinet came off. Lala pulled it out and tossed it on the kitchen floor. She couldn't believe her eyes when she looked back in and saw the door to a safe sitting where the back wall once was. It had a keypad and all. Lala felt around for a way to get the safe out but it was welded into the wall. The only way she was going to be able to penetrate the large steel safe was by way of a combination.

"Damn you, Darell," she mumbled to herself, looking at the keypad. She looked closer at the writing on the safe. It said "4 digit code," at the top of the keypad and instantly Lala's mind started to fill up with possible numbers.

"Mommy, I'm hungry," Tania said, as she banged a couple of pots together on the table.

"I know baby. I'm coming," she answered as she began to punch numbers into the pad.

She was trying everything. Her birthday, Tania's birthday, his birthday, his mom birthday, parts of his social security number, the day that they met, the house number, the code to his email and Facebook, the 4 digit code to their credit cards. She even punched in random numbers hoping it would pop open. It just kept reading incorrect.

"Mommy, I'm hungry," Tania yelled out again, this time throwing one of the pots onto the floor.

It took Lala out of her zone. Tania's cries couldn't be ignored any further. She got down off of the chair, walked over and kissed Tania on the forehead. Then she went over to the stove and began cooking. While preparing the meal the only thing that was on her mind was the safe, so much so that she left the cabinet door open while she cooked just so she could look up at it periodically. She was going to make it her business to get that door open to see what was inside, if it was the last thing she would do.

It seemed like it took forever for the weekend to be over. Lorenzo was looking forward to going to court, especially since Lala said she wasn't going to be there. Lorenzo didn't trust Lala, but he did believe her when she said she not be testifying against him. But today he would find out if she had fed him fact or fiction.

The lawyers were on point with all kinds of petitions for bail in the event the murder charges were dropped. The only thing Lorenzo worried about was the feds. The kind of drug trafficking he was involved with normally grabbed their attention.

"Lorenzo Taylor!" the sheriff yelled out, walking pass the holding cell.

"Yo, right here!" he yelled back, banging on the Plexiglas. "Right here," he said again, getting the sheriff's attention. Lorenzo was pulled out the cell and taken upstairs to the courtroom. When he walked in there weren't a lot of people there, but a smile came over his face when he saw Peanut sitting behind his lawyer. The detainer from his open case had been lifted and Peanut was immediately released. Lorenzo appreciated him coming to court showing his support.

"I see you, playboy," Lorenzo greeted with a salute.

Before he could get into any kind of conversation with him the clerk of the court came in from the judge's chambers. "All Rise!" the man said, as the judge entered the courtroom.

"We have case number 15-213, The State of New York v. Lorenzo Taylor," the judge said, looking down at the pile of papers in front of him. "Has anything changed with the government's status in this matter, particularly the homicide charges?"

"Yes, your Honor. Ms. Johnson is here to testify today," the DA answered.

He turned around and nodded for the sheriff to get Lala from out in the hallway. Lorenzo turned to the back of the courtroom and damn near had a heart attack when Lala walked through the door. He looked over at Peanut who only nodded his head. She walked right past Lorenzo without looking in his direction. *I shoulda had this bitch deaded months ago* Lorenzo thought to himself, shaking his head.

When Lala took the stand she was sworn in by the bailiff and took a seat. The courtroom had an awkward moment of silence as everybody focused on her.

"The state can proceed," the judge said, breaking the silence in the room.

"Thank you your Honor." The DA asked a few basic questions concerning her name and relationship to the deceased. After establishing those facts the DA went to work.

"Ms. Johnson, is the person who killed your daughter's father in the courtroom right now?" the DA asked.

Lala didn't even look at Lorenzo. She simply said, "No," shocking everybody in the courtroom. The DA had to repeat the question again just to make sure she had heard him correctly. Again she answered the question the same. Her response made the DA snap. He started drilling Lala about her previous statement when she said she knew for sure Lorenzo had killed Darell over money. Lala denied everything, saying that the detectives were the ones who made her say those things. Without Lala's cooperation the DA had no other evidence to make the murder charge stick.

"Your Honor, I move to have the charges of murder in the first degree dropped from the State's criminal complaint," Joseph Spear, Lorenzo's attorney, said, standing up.

"I'm in agreement with you, unless the State has other evidence to substantiate the claim of murder," the judge stated, taking off his glasses and giving the DA a look that said, *you fucked up this time.*

Feeling defeated, the DA agreed to drop the murder charges and Lorenzo's lawyers went straight for bail. The judge looked at the paperwork and agreed that a bail could be set for the drug charges, the only thing left on the criminal complaint. The DA tried to object but it was useless.

"Bail is set at one million dollars," the judge said before lowering his gavel. He made the bail high as a favor to the DA, thinking that amount would have Lorenzo stuck behind bars until the trial because he would be unable to come up with the money. Unfortunately for the judge, he had underestimated Lorenzo's pockets. Little did he know, Phenomenon wasn't just sitting in the back of the courtroom for moral support. As soon as bail was set, Phenomenon was out the door.

★

"I see that you're in good company," Erick said, walking out to the deck where Dior and Ms. Ferra were. "You think I can have a word with her, Ms. Ferra?" he asked politely.

Ms. Ferra looked at Dior for approval because she wasn't going anywhere if Dior didn't want her to. Dior nodded her head, letting Ms. Ferra know that it was okay.

"I got my eyes on you," Ms. Ferra snarled before getting up and walking back into the lounge area. Dior shook her head in amusement at Ms. Ferra's comment.

"So what do you wanna talk about?" Dior asked before taking another sip of her lemonade. "I hope you not here to bash my dreams of being a star."

"Nah, and I apologize if you took it that way. I only wanted to open your eyes to something bigger and better."

"See, that's what I don't understand. What do you mean by bigger and better?" Dior huffed.

If Dior really knew who she was talking to, she wouldn't have asked that question. But in a minute she was about to get a crash course on who Erick Marquise Dolphin was.

"When you talkin' about getting back into the industry to do music videos and the cover of men's magazines, that's not being rich and famous, that's being hood rich and local. Outside of New York, people really won't know you."

"Well at least I'll be rich, or hood rich like you call it," Dior responded, rolling her eyes.

"Shit if you call a few thousand dollars in your bank account rich, that's nothin' compared to what I'm talking about. I want you to make real money…long money that can eventually turn into wealth," Erick said with a straight face.

"All that sounds good but I'ma need you to elaborate."

"Let's just say, the kind of money guys like Sway Stone and Phenomenon make in a year, I blow that on my vacations to Paris every summer." Dior's eyes widened in disbelief.

Erick might have been handsome and dressed the part of having his shit together but he damn sure wasn't filthy rich like that, or at least that's what Dior thought.

"How in the hell can you ball out like that on a sponsor salary?" Dior laughed. Erick laughed too, but not with Dior. He was laughing at her for being so closed-minded.

"Listen, I was trying to get you to come off grounds with me the other day so I could introduce you to some people. I think in time you have the potential to be very successful beyond just doing music videos.

"And are you saying this as my sponsor or as a

friend?" Dior said sarcastically.

"I'm doing this as your friend, and maybe one day I might be your boss," he smiled.

"My boss? You still haven't sold me on the idea that you even know what you're talking about."

"Just meet me down by the track tomorrow night at 11:00 and dress to impress," he told Dior before getting up from the table.

Dior was left shaking her head as she watched him walk off the deck. She had to admit that Erick talked a good game, but he was going to have to do more than talking if he was going to convince her. Dior was looking forward to putting him to the test though, to see if Erick was who he said he was.

Chapter 8

Lala sat in the kitchen looking up at the safe's door inside of the cabinet. She tried every code she could think of and the door just wouldn't open. The more she sat there staring the more her brain started to drift off and think about Lorenzo. She was glad she had done the right thing and he would be getting out of jail. Part of her was hoping her good deed would make everything forgiven between the two of them, but knowing Lorenzo's temperament she highly doubted it.

"Mommy! Mommy!" Tania came yelling in the kitchen with a huge smile on her face, shaking Lala out of her thoughts.

"What has you so excited?" Lala said, lifting Tania up.

"Look at the picture I drew for Uncle Lorenzo."

"Isn't this nice," Lala grinned, looking at the crayon drawing of a cake with candles and a little girl, with Tania's name written above it holding hands with a man with the name Uncle Lorenzo above it.

"When can we go visit Uncle Lorenzo again? I want to give him this picture for his birthday."

"Huh…Lorenzo's birthday…what are you talking about, Tania?"

"Remember," Tania looked up at Lala and began rubbing her face. "Uncle Lorenzo's birthday is the day after daddy's."

"That's right, how could I forget. They used to always have a huge birthday party together," Lala mumbled as her mind began racing. "Baby, you go upstairs and start getting ready for bed. I'll be up there shortly to read you a bedtime story."

"Okay, mommy, but hurry."

"I will baby, now give me a kiss. You really are the best little girl in the whole wide world," Lala beamed, before putting her daughter down.

A chill shot through Lala's body. If what she was thinking turned out to be true, then what Tania just told her had changed their lives.

Lala jumped up from the kitchen table, stood on the chair and reached into the cabinet. She said the first four digits of Lorenzo's birthday out loud before punching in the numbers slowly, saying a small prayer while doing so. When she punched in the last number, the safe clicked and the screen read "Access Granted". Lala's heart felt like it exploded when she opened the door and caught sight of the contents inside.

"Damn, Darell," she said pumping her fist in the air before reaching in and pulling out a stack of money.

★

When Eric told Dior that he needed her dressed to impress, he didn't know she was going to go so hard. She had on an off white Balmain 2-split dress and a pair of Dsquared2 6-inch metallic strappy stiletto heels with gold-tone hardware decorated throughout. Her hair was pulled back in a slick bun, bringing out her natural beauty. There was no denying Dior looked amazing and Erick felt honored to be her escort for the night.

"Dior, you're simply stunning."

"Thank you," she blushed. "But when somebody challenges my ability to be a Bad Bitch, I gotta serve extra hard," Dior laughed. "Plus, I wanted to make sure I still had that 'it' factor," she smiled.

"Well you do, and I think being clean makes it shine even more."

Dior did a quick scan of Erick's attire and he still had his signature swag in affect, especially with the iced out Audemars Piguet watch hugging his wrist. He was a little underdressed but Dior was well aware of when somebody was making her their eye candy.

"So who are you tonight and where are you taking me?" Dior asked with a slick grin on her face. Erick looked Dior up and down.

"I'm definitely not your sponsor tonight, and you better pray that we make it to the party," Erick teased as he shook his head, becoming more captivated with what he considered his personal project.

Dior blushed at the way Eric stared at her, like she

was the most precious thing to him. It made her think of Lorenzo and how he used to look at her that very same way. Dior didn't realize how much she craved that from a man until this very moment.

"Nice ride," Dior commented as she sat down in the Limited Edition Aston Martin One-77.

"Glad you approve," Erick smirked before closing Dior's door.

After about 35 to 40 minutes of driving, Erick pulled into a parking garage in the middle of nowhere. Dior must have missed the club on the way in because when she glanced up from getting something out of her purse, she was looking at all kinds of Benzes, Bentleys, Range Rovers and other sports cars she had no idea the names of. The garage was packed with nothing but luxury vehicles.

"Where are we?"

"I told you. We're hanging out with a few of my friends," Erick said, stepping out the car.

As they made their way to the elevator, a thrilling twinge hit Dior. All the fun she used to have hitting the party scene flooded her mind.

"Now stay close to me or you're gonna get lost," Erick said, as the elevator went down.

"What do you mean, stay close?" Dior gave him the side eye. Before Erick could answer the elevator came to a stop and the doors opened.

IF YOU ARE WHO YOU SAY YOU ARE, A SUPER STAR, THEN HAVE NO FEAR THE CAMERA'S HERE Lupa Fiasco was blazing from the speakers when the doors opened.

Dior looked at Erick, who in turn wrapped his arm around her waist and stepped off the elevator with her by his side. The underground club was huge. It had two levels to it with a dance floor the size of a full-length basketball court. It had VIP rooms lined up against the walls and the twin bars downstairs were about 15 yards long. The energy in the building was crazy, something Dior had never seen before at none of the parties she'd been to with Sway or Lorenzo.

"Yo, E!" a white guy yelled out who was sitting on the bar with four models surrounding him.

"Mike, don't hurt yaself!" Erick yelled back as he pointed in his direction.

"Hey Erick, when you wanna move on that?" another man passing by said, before getting lost in the crowd.

"Tony! Call me Monday," Erick yelled back at him. Each step we took towards the VIP section, different people who wanted his attention were hollering at Erick. Dior could see that Erick was somebody of importance to damn near everybody there.

"Damn Erick, you like the president up in here," Dior said, once they got into their VIP section.

"I told you, I'm about bigger and better things Dior," he said, taking a seat next to her in the booth.

Without Erick even ordering anything, the waitress walked over with a crate full to the top on ice. She sat it on the table where Erick reached in and pulled out two bottles of Ace. Dior shot him a look as to remind him that she was still in rehab.

"These ain't for us. It's for our guest," Erick said nodding towards the dance floor. There was an entourage of about six people dancing before walking their way to the VIP area. "This is my team and this is how we get down," Erick smiled, getting up to greet his people.

***

The beat was knocking crazy in the studio. Phenomenon was in the booth spitting mad bars. He made a lot of club music but this time he was going into this gritty, gangsta bag for the people. He was so zoned out on the mic he didn't even see Lorenzo enter the studio. After court, Phenomenon just paid his bail and went right back to work. He had an important meeting with the A&Rs so he couldn't pick Lorenzo up at the jail like he wanted to, but Phenomenon knew they shared the same motto of business first.

"Ahhhh! Dat's my mafuckin' boy," Phenomenon yelled out when he came out the booth from his session.

He walked over and gave Lorenzo a hug along with a few playful jabs to his body. He was happy to see boss man back out on the streets. There was still so much business that had to be dealt with and so much money that needed to be made. Lorenzo was on top of it, though.

"Yo, I can't stay long, homie. I just wanted to come by and check up on you, and let you know that I was out. Thanks for putting that bread..."

"Don't even go there my nigga. Shit, it's yo' money," they laughed. "But I told you, we gone do dis shit to the grave son," Phenomenon said cutting him off. "Nigga, I hope you got some pussy by now though," Phenomenon joked, throwing another playful jab.

"You know I been thinkin' 'bout it."

"Why you gotta think about it? Nigga, you betta just do that shit."

"You know I'm always about my business first. I been away too long and I can't even make no moves on a woman until I get my money shit handled."

"I feel you on that. So that's where you off to now?"

"Yup. I gotta meet with my man Genesis. Get updated on some business shit. But I'ma hit you later on. You just keep puttin' out them hits."

"Got you homie," Phenomenon shot back before going back into the booth.

When Lorenzo arrived at Genesis' penthouse on Central Park West, he was anxious to meet with his business partner so he could get back in the trenches of shit. Lorenzo was so caught up in going over all the things he wanted to discuss with Genesis that it took him a moment to realize the elevator had reopened and someone stepped in. But that quickly changed when a familiar intoxicating scent began to seduce him. It was the perfume Dior always wore and for a brief second Lorenzo's mind started playing tricks on him. He turned to the woman thinking that maybe he would see the face of his lost love again. Right when he was about to speak, Lorenzo snapped out of his delusions.

"Is there a problem?" the woman asked, feeling some type of way at how the stranger was staring at her.

"I apologize. I thought you were somebody I knew."

"Oh really…is that the best you can do?"

"I'm serious. It was your perfume. A woman I once knew always wore it. It was her favorite."

"That woman has excellent taste. This perfume is not only very expensive but also very exclusive."

"I know. I was the one that bought it for her." At that moment the elevator doors opened and both began to make their exit at the same time. "I apologize, ladies first," Lorenzo said, stepping back so the woman could get off.

"Thank you." As they both walked down the hall they ended up in front of the same door. "Are you a friend of Genesis?" the woman asked before ringing the doorbell.

"Yes, I am. My name is Lorenzo."

"Nice to meet you. I'm Precious," the woman said, extending her hand.

"If it isn't two of my favorite people," Genesis said, greeting his guests after opening the door. "Please come in."

"I met your friend Lorenzo on our way up. Where have you been hiding him?"

"Lorenzo is a busy man. Unfortunately I don't get

to see him as much as I like."

"Whatever, man. We're both busy but when we are able to get together it's all love."

"Well I'm not going to interfere on you all's time. Knowing Genesis I'm sure you all have important business to handle. But I needed to drop off these papers that Quentin wanted you to have. After you go over them call me if you have any questions."

"Will do. Thanks," Genesis said, taking the envelope from Precious.

"Lorenzo, it was a pleasure meeting you. Make sure you let that woman know that she's lucky to have a man with such great taste in perfume. Bye." Lorenzo and Genesis both watched as Precious left out the front door before speaking.

"What was that about?" Genesis inquired, before pouring a drink for himself and Lorenzo.

"Just a brief conversation we had on the elevator. But wow, that woman is beautiful."

"And very married."

"I did notice that huge rock on her finger. And since I know you're not married then she must be somebody else's wife. Is he a friend of yours?"

"No, he's not, but Nico, the father of his wife's daughter is a very good friend of mine and one of my business partners."

"Is that your way of telling me she's off limits?" Lorenzo asked, taking a sip of his drink.

"I would think the ring on her finger would tell you that."

"True, but when you have the pleasure of meeting a woman like that, you have to ask."

Dior wouldn't have believed in a million years that Erick was a behind the scenes movie producer. He had his hands in some of the biggest films out right now. Not only was he a movie producer, he also was the owner of the Rockview Rehabilitation Center. He wasn't just rich, he was wealthy. He went around the room introducing his team, which consisted of his hair and make-up specialists, Tina and Ashley who were both middle-aged white women.

Then there was Malisa Macht, a one-woman legal team herself. She did a lot of the cleanup work when lawsuits came into play. Based on her last name and her facial features, Dior assumed she was Jewish. Fats was his personal security on days Erick felt like he needed it. Fats was a white marine jug head who did eight years in Iraq before he lost his marbles. He got rehabilitated at Rockview, then ended up getting a job for Erick later on. David and Joe were Erick's business partners in producing movies.

David was Jewish and Joe was Italian and both were film negotiating experts. Come to find out, just about everybody in the club had something to do with the movie business, whether they were actors, producers, directors, writers or of course groupies. Dior just sat there taking it all in.

"Hey Dave!" Erick yelled over the music. "I want you to find Tony and set up a meeting with him tomorrow. Tell him I might have found somebody to play that part."

Tony was also a producer, but he did sitcom shows that ended up on BET or Lifetime. He had recently asked Erick if he knew somebody that was willing to play a small role in one of his shows. When most of the producers in the film industry wanted to find talented black actresses, they went to Erick, and that's just what Tony did. It didn't dawn on Erick until a few days ago that Dior might be a good fit.

"Who'd you have in mind?" Dave questioned, raising the bottle of Ace to his mouth. Erick looked over at Dior who was sitting there still mesmerized by the scene. He then looked back over at Dave.

Dior didn't have the slightest idea what was about to be placed in her lap. It was one of those golden opportunities that many people heard about but few ever experienced. With a little hard work and some coaching from Erick it was possible Dior could achieve the fame she had always desired.

Chapter 9

Lorenzo had been home for a few months and by this time word had spread throughout every borough in NYC. Everybody that owed him money had been waiting for him when he came to collect because they knew now that Lorenzo was out of jail, he would once again dominate the streets. Even while fighting drug charges by the state of New York, Lorenzo remained in the game real heavy. Besides dibbing and dabbing in the music industry, the game was all he knew. He was good at it too, besides dealing with a weak nigga that turned informant.

Lorenzo was on the verge of finding out who that was. He pulled up and parked in front of the bodega and beeped his horn twice. A few minutes later a Puerto Rican chick came out of the store. She was gorgeous too. Anytime Lorenzo saw her she always reminded him of Regan Gomez Preston, except that her hair was longer and her skin complexion was a couple shades lighter.

"¿Como Esta?" Lorenzo greeted as she got into

the car.

"Nigga, don't be trying to talk that Spanish shit to me. When da hell did you get out and why da fuck didn't you call me?" she snapped.

"Carmen, you know how busy I be. I had to take care of a lot of...hold up! Hold up! Why the hell am I explaining myself to you?" he chuckled.

Carmen chuckled too, leaning over and giving Lorenzo a kiss. Carmen was like Lorenzo's best-kept secret. She wasn't his girl, but in both of their own little worlds they were like Mr. and Mrs. Smith. Aside from her good looks Carmen was an animal when it came down to that murder game. She had more homicides under her belt then anybody in the city and she did it all like a paid assassin. She moved with a quiet swiftness so her victims never knew she was coming. Flat out, Carmen was vicious and the only person in the world who knew her hidden talent was Lorenzo. That's because he taught her everything she knew.

"Look, I need you to take care of something for me," Lorenzo said, reaching into his center console and pulling out a yellow envelope with money in it.

"I'm listening," she responded, stuffing the envelope in her back pocket.

"Do you remember the bitch Alexus I had workin' for me not too long ago?"

"Yeah, I remember her. She was the one who thought she had you. Dumb bitch!" Carmen said rolling her eyes.

"Look at you getting all jealous," Lorenzo smiled.

"You know I'm not gonna let nobody take your place. Hey, if it makes you feel any better, I need you to take her off count," Lorenzo said, putting the hit in play.

Lorenzo knew that once he let Carmen off the leash Alexus was as good as dead. Carmen never missed once she got the green light on somebody. It didn't matter where Alexus was or how good she was trying to stay under the radar, Carmen was going to find her and when she did it was lights out.

"It'll be my fuckin' pleasure," Carmen said, leaning over and giving Lorenzo another kiss before she got out of the car. Lorenzo could see the look in Carmen's eyes as she walked in front of the car to go back into the store. She was locked in and he knew she was going straight to work.

Brittani drove through the countryside, top down in an all-white Mercedes-Benz SL 500. The sun was shining bright so a pair of peach-colored tinted Gucci frames covered her eyes as she sped down the desolate road. She still hadn't gotten used to seeing this side of New York, considering the only time she had been out of the city was to visit her family that lived in Virginia. She drove by farms that had cows and horses grazing in large pieces of land. In the 75 miles of driving all she saw were trees and grassland. The fresh air was a far cry from the smell of fast food restaurants and gas guzzling vehicles she was used to.

After hours of driving, Brittani pulled into the large rehabilitation center that sat on what appeared to be an enormous estate. The main building mirrored a Country French-Style Mansion with a huge parking lot for both the employees and visitors. Getting on the premises was a process in itself. Security was tight, so tight that by the time Brittani got out of her car a guard was there to check her credentials before escorting her over to the main building.

"Hello, how can I help you?" the receptionist asked, poking her head up from her computer.

"Yes I'm here to see..." Brittani stopped mid-sentence as she looked over and saw Dior walking up the steps to the main building. She couldn't control her excitement over seeing Dior for the first time in months.

"Haaayyyy!" Brittani smiled, as she ran over to Dior with open arms.

"Hi Brittani," Dior beamed, giving her a hug. "It took you long enough," she playfully stated, wiping the tear that was falling down her cheek.

The last person Dior had seen from NYC before checking into the rehab facility was Brittani. So seeing a familiar face was exactly what Dior needed.

"Damn girl, this place look nice," Brittani said, as they walked outside towards the recreational area.

"Yeah, it should be for how much it cost."

"As beautiful as this place is, I'm not surprised," Brittani commented, taking in the scenery.

"Yeah, it's beautiful and peaceful. It's probably the reason I've been here for months but I still don't want to leave."

"Hell, I don't blame you. From the looks of it, it seems like a never ending vacation."

"Something like that, but it's also keeping me from dealing with life. We both know that in real life it's not a never ending vacation."

"True indeed. Speaking of dealing with real life, are you all allowed to look at the news?"

"Yes, silly. We have televisions in our rooms. Why do you ask?"

Brittani looked at Dior with a raised eyebrow. "So does that mean you heard about Sway?" she questioned, before digging into her bag, and pulling out the newspaper from last week.

Truth was, Dior was so caught up in her treatment, she really didn't have time to watch much television and she had no clue what was going on in the streets. Dior felt that the more she cut herself off from her previous life, the quicker she would make a full recovery. When Brittani passed her the paper Sway's face was on the front page, and under his picture read the words "Hip Hop Icon Murdered."

"Sway is dead," Dior stated in an unexpectedly calm voice. Dior repeated what she had said, not as if she wanted confirmation but more so in disbelief.

"Are you okay? Do you need to sit down?" Brittani questioned, taking Dior's hand.

"I'm fine."

"Are you sure?" Brittani asked, as if she didn't quite believe her friend.

"Yes I'm sure. I guess Sway's death is somewhat surreal to me. I've been spending months in rehab trying to figure out why I was drawn to the life I shared with him. I knew with every line I snorted and every pill I popped I could possibly be knocking on death's door but yet I kept going back. No matter how strong I felt, part of me feared leaving this facility because I wasn't sure if I could withstand the temptation if I saw Sway again. But now he's dead, so I can no longer use him as an excuse for hiding out up here."

"Dior, you're not hiding, you're getting better. And I'm not a psychiatrist but I think it's natural to have those fears. It might even be a good thing because it will make you more cautious, to not put yourself in the same situations that got you here."

"I never would wish death on anybody but I'm glad Sway is gone. He was like poison for me, so I can't help but think that he deserved whatever he got. Does that make me a bad person?" Dior asked as she sat down on one of the benches around the pond.

"No, it makes you human." Dior turned towards Brittani and smiled.

"Brittani, I've been making so much progress and my sponsor Erick has been incredible to me. Not only is he super rich but he's also involved in the movie industry and he wants to help me accomplish all my dreams. The thing is, as much as I want it I'm so afraid."

"What are you afraid of?"

"Having to fight the temptation of the drugs. You know once I'm in the business again I'll be surrounded by that lifestyle. Resisting that temptation is going to be so difficult."

"It will, but I have confidence in you. You've shown time and time again that once you put your mind to something you can make it happen. You were willing to give up everything to get clean and you did it."

"Yeah, and it's cost me the only man I've ever truly loved"

"You mean Lorenzo. I know leaving him was difficult but you had to save yourself, Dior. He's locked up. There's nothing he can do for you. Staying clean and getting your life back on track is what's most important. If Erick can make that happen for you then you should go for it."

"You're right. But if I do pursue my career again Lorenzo will eventually discover that I'm very much alive. For some reason in my mind, I figured that Lorenzo would end up spending the rest of his life behind bars and I would grow old in some remote little town never seeing him again. I didn't consider that after I became drug-free that I would still want to obtain fame and fortune."

"Girl you can't worry about Lorenzo right now. You have to do you. They say opportunity only knocks once; well it's knocking a second time for you, so you better answer.

Dior thought about what Brittani was saying. She knew where her friend was coming from, but that didn't ease the pain of missing Lorenzo. She yearned to have him back in her life more than anything. She was beginning to regret the lie she had fabricated, but at the time Dior truly believed it was her best option. Now she wasn't so sure. What scared Dior more than anything was Lorenzo learning the truth and hating her for it. The very idea of that made Dior's eyes fill with tears.

There was one person Lorenzo couldn't stop thinking about since he'd been home. His life didn't feel right without Dior in it. Right about now all he wanted to do was pay his respects by visiting her grave. He felt that was the least he could do since he couldn't make it to her funeral. Lorenzo got out of his car and walked up the driveway to Courtney's house. When she answered the door she damn near shitted on herself at the sight of him.

"Lorenzo, when did you get out?" she asked nervously.

"A few months ago. I would've come seen you sooner but you moved and I had a hard time tracking you down. How have you been?"

"I'm, I'm, doin' okay I guess. Wow, it's nice to see you back out," Courtney lied. The word was Lorenzo was going to spend the rest of his life in jail. Courtney, or anybody else that knew him, never would have thought he'd be back on the streets.

"So where is she?" Lorenzo asked, stumping Courtney with the question. "Where's Dior?" He looked serious when he asked so she didn't know if he was talking about Dior being dead or alive.

Did he know that Dior faked her death and ran away to a rehab? Courtney thought to herself.

"Listen, I'm just tryna pay my respect," Lorenzo said, in a more non-threatening manner.

She looked at the sadness in his face and started to regret going this far with the lie. While Lorenzo was locked up, Courtney took it upon herself to ask Lorenzo to pay for the funeral cost. She only did it because she was broke at the time, but Lorenzo accommodated her and gave her twenty-five thousand dollars so that Dior could have the proper burial. Courtney ended up blowing the money on bullshit. She lied and told Lorenzo that Dior had an intimate yet lovely funeral with only family and a few close friends. Courtney did that even after Dior told her to tell Lorenzo that she was cremated. But once Courtney told one lie the rest just rolled off her tongue with ease, that is until now.

"Well I'm kind of busy right now Lorenzo, so I can't take you out there at this moment. If you call me tomorrow I can..."

"Nah that's cool. You can just tell me where she's at and I'll go by myself," Lorenzo said, cutting her off.

"Even if I told you where she's buried you wouldn't be able to find her. Like I told you before, she buried in a secluded place. Your money was well spent," Courtney shot back.

Lorenzo bit the bottom of his lip in frustration. He really wanted to visit Dior at her gravesite but it seemed as though it wasn't going to happen today. He looked at Courtney and nodded his head, then went back to his callous ways.

"You right. Make sure you answer your phone when I call you tomorrow. I don't care how busy you are, make yaself unbusy. A'ight," he said, not even giving her the chance to answer him as he walked off back down the steps and to his car.

Courtney stood at the door stuck, and it was at this very moment she knew that she had bitten off more than she could chew.

Chapter 10

"So, what are you going to do after next week?" Erick asked Dior as he passed her the towel after she stepped out of the pool.

"I'm not really sure yet. I guess I'ma go back home and clean my apartment first," she joked. "Why, you got a job for me, Mr. Big Time Producer?" she smiled.

"What if I told you I set you up with an interview so you can convince some of my friends that you're ready to play a small role on the television show Baller Chicks?" Erick said, with a big smile on his face.

"Come on Erick, stop playing with me," Dior responded, doubtful the television world was ready for somebody like her, especially coming straight out of rehab.

"Well that night I took you out, all of my associates were very impressed. If you had been paying attention you would have noticed all eyes were on you."

"Seriously?" Dior asked, brightening up her attitude.

"I'm dead serious. Look Dior, I'm not gonna lie, I made some moves for you and that's because I think you have what it takes. You're young, beautiful, smart and if I can say so myself, you have an amazing body," Erick said, unable to stop staring at how good Dior looked in her bikini. I just wanna give you a chance to make major moves. All you gotta do is show up to the interview and the part is pretty much yours."

Dior couldn't hold back her excitement any longer. "Yesss!" she screamed at the top of her lungs. "I'll do it!"

"That's all I needed to hear," Erick smiled.

"Thank you! Thank you! Thank you!" Dior said, giving him a bunch of playful pecks to his lips. "Really though, Erick. Thank you," Dior said in a soft tone, looking him directly in his eyes.

It was at that very instant they both had a moment. Erick wanted to lean in and kiss Dior but he resisted the urge. Instead he imagined what it would be like for their lips to meet. He wanted his tongue to gently swipe against her soft lips and taste every part of her.

"What y'all doing over here?" Ms. Ferra said, interrupting Erick's daydreaming as she walked up on them in the pool area.

"Erick was just sharing some really great news with me. I need to go change but I'll fill you in later on," Dior told Ms. Ferra, as she wrapped the towel around her waist and walked off. Ms. Ferra waited until Dior was out of sight before she spoke.

"You know Erick, that's a nice girl and I like her.

So don't be selling her the same dreams you sold some of these other girls that didn't know any better," Ms. Ferra cautioned, walking up on him.

Ms. Ferra knew Erick very well and watched how he used his status to get women in bed and then break their hearts. He made promises he never meant to keep and his charm was damn near irresistible. She didn't want that for Dior. Not at this point in her life when she had come so far.

"I'm not selling her no dreams, and whether you believe me or not, I really do like her," Erick admitted. "I know you might hate me because of what my father did to you,"....Smackkk! Ms. Ferra went across his face with the brown side of her hand.

"Don't you ever...in ya natural born life disrespect me," Ms. Ferra warned through clenched teeth, and then walked away.

"I'm not him!" Erick yelled as he watched Ms. Ferra disappear through the double doors. She didn't even pay him any mind. Erick just sat on the bleachers rubbing the side of his face where Ms. Ferra slapped him.

★

Brice walked into the crib to find Alexus pacing back and forth in the living room. She looked scared to death, which made Brice concerned.

"Yo, what ma?" Brice asked, stepping right in the middle of her path. She stopped in front of him, looked up at him and spoke.

"He's home," Alexus said, turning around to finish pacing.

"Who da fuck is you talkin' about?" Brice barked, becoming irritated by the pacing.

"It's Zo. Zo is home," she said again, this time getting all of Brice's attention.

"What you mean Zo is home?" he yelled, walking up to Alexus.

"I thought you said the nigga was finished."

"I thought he was. I don't know what happened," Alexus shot back with an attitude. "All I know is that I'm not leaving this house," she said, pulling the 9mm from her back pocket and checking to make sure she had a bullet in the chamber.

Brice was a little upset that Alexus was shook like this. She made him feel like he wasn't man enough to protect her from Lorenzo. In his eyes Alexus was somewhat of his woman now and as far as he was concerned, it was whatever.

"Maaan fuck Lorenzo," Brice spit as he watched Alexus go over to the table and sniff a line of coke. "Yo, and stop putting dat shit up ya nose. I thought you said you was going to slow down."

"I am, I'm just stressed da fuck out right now. Dis nigga is gonna kill me," she whined, walking back over to the table where the coke was at.

She didn't use no straw or no dollar bill, she leaned over, stuck her nose into the 1 ½ ounces of powder on the table and took a quick sniff. Brice looked at her like she was crazy. He proceeded towards her with caution seeing that she still had the gun in her hand. He got right up to her and slowly took the gun out of her hand.

"Yo ma, he's not gonna kill you," Brice spoke in a low tone. I'ma go out here find Zo and try to straighten dis shit out. If he get crazy and act like he want some drama, I'ma blow da nigga head off," he said, wiping the cocaine residue from her nose.

Brice took the 9mm and tucked in into his waist. He kissed Alexus on her forehead, then on her lips, calming her down somewhat. She was actually beginning to feel safe with him trying to step up and be her protector. She reached up and gave him another kiss before he turned and headed for the door.

"Be careful," Alexus said, before walking over to clean the cocaine off the table.

Brice smiled looking back at her as he opened the door. When he turned to leave he walked into Carmen's gun that was pointed at his forehead. She squeezed the trigger, double tapping it so that two hot lead balls pierced his skull, killing him instantly. Hearing the two shots, Alexus turned but all she could see was Brice's body falling to the ground. She wasted no time in taking off running towards the bedroom.

Carmen stood at the door, firing round after round at her, barely missing Alexus who shot down the hallway. Carmen stepped over Brice's body dropping the empty clip from her gun and popping in a fresh one. Alexus ran to her bedroom and slammed the door behind her. She didn't know what to do.

"Oh shit! Oh shit!" she mumbled to herself,

looking around the room.

Carmen walked down the narrow hallway with both hands cupped around the gun with it pointed in front of her at shoulder's length. The first door she came to was a bathroom door, which she didn't even look in. She just stuck the gun inside and let off several rounds blindly before peeking inside. Alexus jumped from the sound of the gun being fired. She looked around the room and thankfully remembered that Brice kept a gun under the mattress. She ran over and jumped behind the king size bed, reaching in between the mattress and feeling around for the gun. Pop! Pop! Pop! Carmen fired three shots into the bedroom door that was parallel to the bed.

Alexus dipped down but continued to feel around for the gun until she found it. She pulled it out, took the safety off and began squeezing the trigger into the direction of the door. Pow! Pow! Pow! Pow! Carmen dipped away from the door in the nick of time, sending a couple of more shots back at Alexus. The gunfire from Alexus surprised the hell out of Carmen. If Alexus was in the room with a gun it was going to be almost impossible for Carmen to get to her without walking into the line of fire. She didn't even know how much ammo Alexus had in the room with her.

"Damn!" Carmen said, after hearing police sirens in the distance coming towards the apartment complex.

She wanted to stay and finish the job but the longer she stood there the closer the sirens got. She looked down the hallway at the bedroom door, then back over at Brice's dead body in the doorway. She definitely didn't want to be there when the cops showed up with his body lying there. This was Carmen's first time leaving behind a breathing victim. Coming up short on her assignment wasn't sitting well with her either as she rolled her eyes at the bedroom door before walking out of the apartment. She put an extra two bullets in the back of Brice's head on her way out, then dropped the murder weapon on his back so that she wouldn't be leaving with any evidence on her.

"Damn, playboy. I'm glad you could make it," Phenomenon said, jumping up from his chair when Lorenzo walked onto the set. "It's crazy bitches in here, dog."

"I see," Lorenzo replied, looking around at all the young, beautiful women walking back and forth. "You gone have all these ladies in ya video?"

"Oh nah, bro. This is just auditions. Only four of these broads gone make it," Phenomenon responded, looking around at ass and tits everywhere.

Being around all these video chicks made Lorenzo start thinking about Dior and how she put 95% of these women to shame when it came down to body and looks. She would have been one of the four females for sure.

"So you looking forward to this weekend…I know I am," Phenomenon said, playfully punching Lorenzo's arm. "You know we gotta do it big. And you know I gotta put on for you."

Phenomenon was talking about the party he was

throwing Lorenzo. It was a coming home party and a belated birthday party. Both had actually taken place months ago but this was the first time their schedules permitted a proper celebration. He was going to shut down the 40/40 Club for the whole night, and that was big considering it was the 4th of July weekend. Only chicks with pretty faces and fat asses were allowed in. If you were a dude, you had to know Lorenzo personally or be cool with somebody in his clique. Other than that, you had to stand outside.

"Actually I am too. I need to try and enjoy myself. I've dealt wit' so much bad shit over the last few months, it's time for something good."

"Oh damn, homie, I forgot to tell you that I'm sorry I couldn't make it to Dior's funeral. By the time I heard about her death they told me she was already in the ground," Phenomenon said, figuring some of the bad shit Lorenzo was speaking of was his lady love. "You know Shawty would have been in my video," he smiled.

"Yea that's crazy. I...Hold up, is that the chick Courtney?" Lorenzo asked, changing the subject when he saw a female that resembled Courtney sitting amongst the group of women.

He excused himself from Phenomenon and walked over to her, squeezing his way through the crowd of women. When she turned from talking to one of the girls, she was shocked to see Lorenzo standing there.

"Oh hey, Lorenzo," she greeted him with a fake smile.

"What up Courtney. Can I speak to you over here

for a minute?" he asked, taking her by the hand and walking her away from the other females. "I got caught up in handling some business so I wasn't able to hit you the next day but you didn't forget about what I said, did you?"

"You know I wouldn't forget about you, Lorenzo. If you want, we can go right after the audition. I really don't have anything to do and plus I gotta put some fresh flowers on Dior's grave," Courtney told him. He couldn't even get mad at her because she was willing to take him out to the gravesite on sight.

"Yea yea, that's cool, but let's do it tomorrow. That works better for me. I'ma be here for the auditions anyway so we can discuss what time to link up after you're done."

"Hey Lorenzo," Courtney said, stopping him before he walked off. "You think you can put a good word in with Phenomenon for one of the feature spots?" she asked, looking around at all the female competition.

Lorenzo looked Courtney up and down. She was standing there in a pair of Juicy Couture shorts, a tank top and some wedges. Her body did make that basic outfit look sexy as hell, not to mention she was also very attractive. Even without a word from Lorenzo, she had a decent shot at getting one of the spots on her own.

"Yeah, sure Courtney. I'll holla at him for you," Lorenzo said and walked off.

Chapter 11

When Dior walked into the office just about everybody's jaws dropped. Every inch of her inevitable curves were on full blast thanks to the Helmut Lang maxi dress Erick got for her. The asymmetrical hemline and figure-flattering draping accentuated her body to perfection. Her jet-black hair cascaded down her shoulders, perfectly highlighting the golden chain-link necklace. In fact, Dior already looked like a star and she knew it.

After all the introductions and the shaking of hands, Dior took a seat at the long, brown cedar wood table with everybody, including Erick, who sat next to her.

"Okay Dior, tell me in ten words or less why I should give you this role," Tony said, looking to get a quick answer.

"I'll make people watch the show," she answered without hesitation.

He said ten words and she gave him six strong

words that made the biggest impact. It kind of blew everybody's mind when she said it, and judging by the way every man and woman looked at her, when she entered the room what she said actually made sense.

Tony didn't even have to consult with the rest of his team on the matter. He sat up in his chair and crossed his hands on the table. Everybody in the room was quiet but Erick, who already knew what was about to be said.

"We have to do a little paperwork, sign a few contracts and of course cut you a check, but I think it's safe to say that you got the part," Tony said, looking around the room at his colleagues who were nodding in agreement.

Dior wanted to scream at the top of her lungs but decided to be a little more professional. She only screamed on the inside.

"Thank you Tony. I give you my word, you won't regret this move," Dior said, standing up, reaching over and shaking his hand.

"A'ight, now get her out of my office before I make this girl a permanent fixture," he joked, tapping Erick on his shoulder. And just like that, Dior got the role and Tony was on to other pending business.

★

When Lorenzo arrived at Daniel on E. 65th Street he was looking forward to sitting down for some of their world-renowned French cuisine. It had always been one of his favorite spots, but Lorenzo had been running the streets nonstop since getting out of jail, so this was his first time having a moment to come sit down for an excellent meal.

"Mr. Taylor, follow me," the hostess said, taking him to his table.

"Lorenzo, right?" a woman said, stopping him on his way to sit down.

"Yes."

"You have good taste in perfume and restaurants."

"Thank you, and your name is Precious, correct?"

"That's correct. I guess we both remember names very well."

"Or maybe we both just remember people who interest us." Precious gave him a slight smile. That simple gesture was all the incentive Lorenzo needed. "Have you already eaten?"

"No. Actually I was supposed to be meeting my daughter but she just called and had to cancel. So I was on my way out."

"There's no reason for you to leave. I'm here alone and would love for you to join me."

"Are you sure?"

"Positive."

For the next few hours Lorenzo and Precious were engrossed in a deep conversation. They were so caught up in listening to each other they barely touched their food. Lorenzo found Precious completely fascinating and hadn't felt this drawn to a woman since the first time he'd laid eyes on Dior.

"We've been talking for hours and you've discussed your childhood, the impact the death of your mother had on you, finding your father and countless stories about your kids. The only person you haven't discussed is your husband."

Precious glanced down at her ring finger and then stared back up at Lorenzo. "I guess it is pretty obvious I'm a married woman."

"Yes, with the size of that ring there is no hiding it. But I still have to ask, why haven't you mentioned your husband, not even once?"

"I've been with my husband for the majority of my adult life. We've been to hell and back a few times, but through it all I always believed we would end up together, but…"

"But what?"

"But now I'm not sure. He's so distant emotionally, physically and he's hardly ever home. It's like he would rather be anywhere else but with me. He doesn't seem to love me anymore," Precious said solemnly. Lorenzo could hear the pain in her voice and he didn't understand how any man could stop loving a woman like her.

"I doubt that," he said, reaching over touching her hand. "I'm sure your husband still loves you very much. I've never been married but all people go through hard times in their relationships. It doesn't mean the love is gone."

"Thank you. I wasn't expecting for you to say that."

"Neither was I," Lorenzo gave a subtle laugh. "Precious, I'm sure you know that I'm extremely attracted to you. I have been since we first met on the elevator. But I would never try to make you question the love I'm sure your husband has for you in order to get you. With that being said, it doesn't change the fact that I do want you."

"I love how direct you are. That trait makes you even more appealing."

Precious didn't know it, but at that moment Lorenzo decided married or not, he had to have her. Dior was the only woman who had ever stimulated his mind, body and soul. Lorenzo didn't think it was possible any other woman could ever have that effect on him, until now.

***

"What you lookin' at?" Erick glanced over and asked Dior, who was curled up in the passenger seat with her shoes off.

"I'm looking at you," she smiled. "I was thinking about how that celibacy thing was going for you."

"Really," Erick said, glancing over at Dior then back out at the road.

"You were saying you were waiting for that right person to come along."

"Yeah, yeah. I made a vow to myself to stay celibate until I find the right person who I want to be in a committed relationship with. I need a partner, someone I can trust, confide in with anything that's going on in my life. I want somebody that can be my equal, and when it comes down to my heart I want her to be able to protect it from getting hurt. I..."

Erick's cell started ringing, interrupting what he was saying. He reached over and looked at the screen to see that Dave was calling. Dior shot him a look like he'd better not answer it and mess up the mood. She was enjoying hearing what he wanted in a relationship.

"I gotta take this. Give me two minutes. I'm sure it's about you," he said, then answered. "Yo what's good?"

"Yo, I just got off the phone with Tony and that paperwork we were going over yesterday, he needs me to bring it to his office. The thing is, I left it at your crib and I'm in the city," Dave explained.

"Say no more. I can shoot over there and then meet Tony at the office in less than an hour," Erick said, looking up at the street signs to see where he was.

"Appreciate it," Dave said before Erick hung up the phone. He turned off on the next street to head towards his house, which was only about 15 minutes away.

When they pulled up to Erick's mansion Dior had to sit up in her seat as the winding driveway led to the French renaissance-style mansion. "Wow, this is your house?"

"Yup."

"I'm speechless, and that's a rarity for me," Dior laughed.

"True indeed. Would you like to take a look inside?"

"I hope you didn't think I was gonna wait out here in the car. Of course I want to see the inside," Dior popped, anxious to see what was behind the double doors.

When they went inside, the interior did not disappoint. The stunning two-story entrance with black walnut parquet floors mesmerized Dior. From the marble staircase, cathedral living room with stone fireplace, the ornate dining room with tracery ceiling and oak columns, the wood paneled library and the wine cellar, no detail was missed or expense spared. The home was simply marvelous.

"Where does this elevator lead?"

"The second floor master suite. Let's take a ride up."

"Sure."

When they arrived on the second floor, a massive balcony the length of the entire floor with serene views greeted them.

"I think I'm in love," Dior said, becoming hypnotized as she stared out watching the sunset from the balcony.

"So do I," Erick countered, taking Dior in his arms, and before she could say a word his tongue was down her throat. Her body willingly gave into the caress of his hands, the softness of his lips and the wetness of his mouth. She found herself following Erick's lead as he led her to his bed, which seemed to become more inviting as each of his touches seduced her even further.

Erick gently laid Dior on the bed and climbed on top of her, slowly slipping off her dress. Dior then pulled Erick's shirt over his head, revealing his well-carved chest. He sat up and looked down on her body. He let his hand glide over her breast then down the center of her stomach till he reached her thighs. He leaned over and kissed her stomach before going further down, till his warm kisses landed on her clit. Dior arched her back, reached down and grabbed the back of his head. Erick kissed and licked then sucked on her clit. He reversed the process by sucking, licking and kissing it again.

"Mmmmmm!" Dior moaned in pleasure, as her body gave into what it had been missing for so long. Erick pushed his tongue in deeper and sucked on her pussy at the same time as Dior latched onto the sheets, almost pulling them off. Her body locked up and Erick could feel the inside of her pussy tighten up as the wetness filled his mouth. His tongue work made it clear that Erick wanted to taste every bit of her.

"Ohhh Yesss! Ohhh Yesss!" Dior yelled out as her body started shivering all over. "Ohhh Yesss, Lorenzo! I love you baby," Dior continued without realizing she was screaming another man's name.

That shit right there shut the mood down in seconds. Erick's dick went front rock hard to damn near limp. The pussy that a moment ago had the sweetest taste in the world and made Erick feel powerful now seemed like kryptonite.

"Who the fuck is Lorenzo!" The anger and disgust in Erick's voice was apparent.

It took Dior a minute to respond. Although she knew Lorenzo constantly remained on her mind, she was taken aback that she had called his name while being intimate with another man. "Erick, I'm so sorry," Dior said, reaching for the blanket. She wanted to cover her body as if hiding from shame.

"Fuck being sorry! I'm trying to make love to you but you screamin' out the next man's name. What type of shit is that!" Erick yelled, as he started putting back on his clothes. "And you still haven't told me who he is."

"He's the man I mentioned to you a few months

ago."

"Oh, the man who cheated on you and in jail. So you have a good man who wants to treat you right standing in your face but you cryin' out for some no good nigga."

"Lorenzo is a good man!"

"If he's such a good man, then why isn't he here with you? That's right, he's locked up."

"So what if he's locked up! Good men go to jail all the time," Dior shot back, becoming defensive at how Erick was trying to make it seem that Lorenzo was less than.

"Yeah, and you can write letters, send emails, and make phone calls while locked up. It doesn't seem like he's made any effort to see how you're doing. If he were a real man he would still make sure you're straight even behind bars. So what's his excuse for that?"

"Because he thinks I'm dead!" Dior belted, instantly regretting that she let that information slip out of her mouth.

"Dead?" Erick questioned as if he misunderstood what she said.

"Yes, dead. When I decided to get clean he was in jail and I thought he would be there for the rest of his life. I figured I was doing the best thing for us both if he believed I had died."

"If you thought it was better for him to believe you were dead instead of being in your life, there's a reason. I'm saying that as your sponsor not as your lover."

Dior looked down at her hands and began rubbing

her fingers together nervously before glancing back up to meet Erick's glare. "Maybe you're right. But now I realize that until I get closure with Lorenzo, I can't be with you or anybody else."

Courtney and Lorenzo pulled into the St. John's Cemetery in Albany, New York where Courtney told Lorenzo they had buried Dior. Courtney had her scheme game intact though. She came here the very next day after Lorenzo had shown up at her crib expectantly and brought a plot far off in the back of the cemetery for a few hundred dollars. She gave the director of the cemetery a long story about how her friend died in a brutal house fire but was never afforded a proper burial because she didn't have any family. She told them that the body was cremated so there wasn't any need to dig a hole. She basically told him she wanted a place to come to remember her friend. Not only did the director believe her, for an extra 500.00 he gave her a small tombstone with Dior's name engraved on it.

"Damn, why y'all got her all the way back here?" Lorenzo asked as he walked behind Courtney.

"I wanted Dior to have her own little section back here away from everybody else. She always stood out from the crowd," Courtney said, as she walked up to the tombstone that read Dior's name.

Lorenzo walked up to the tombstone and looked around. It was in a secluded area away from everybody else. Lorenzo had never buried anybody and the plot and location could've been perceived as something exclusive and reserved for a person that had some money. However, Lorenzo did find a few things odd.

"A lot of people adored Dior; I'm surprised there aren't any flowers on her tombstone."

"I normally bring some with me but today I forgot. I'll be sure to bring some back out here the next time I come," Courtney said, trying to clean up her mistake.

Lorenzo didn't say anything, he just took a mental note of it, along with everything else he noticed that was questionable about the gravesite. Like the location of the cemetery, the place of the plot, the fresh dirt that was around the tombstone. Lorenzo took it all in. He couldn't put his finger on it quite yet but his gut told him something wasn't right. Once he wrapped up other pertinent business matters in his life, Lorenzo was going to get a clear understanding about what exactly happened to Dior.

Chapter 12

Lorenzo looked over and smiled when Carmen got into the car with a pouty but angry look on her face. It was due to the fact she was unable to kill Alexus in the apartment the other day. Lorenzo found it amusing that Carmen was so upset. He knew it was eating her up on the inside.

"What are you smiling about?" Carmen said, cutting her eyes over and seeing Lorenzo looking at her.

"Awweee! Da baby missed," he teased playfully as he reached over and pinched her cheeks.

"I don't feel like playin' wit you," she shot back, pulling away from his hand.

"Shut up and get ya ass over here," he smiled, grabbing her by the back of her neck and pulling her towards him.

It didn't matter how mad she was, Carmen, just like a lot of women, couldn't resist Lorenzo. She climbed over into the driver side, straddling him while he leaned his seat back. He reached under her mini skirt and palmed her ass with both of his hands causing Carmen to become aroused. The frown on her face began to fade away at his touch.

"You really shot that nigga in his head?" Lorenzo asked, looking up at her.

Carmen nodded her head in affirmation, leaning down and pressing her lips up against his. She was sexy as hell to Lorenzo, especially since he knew that she was a stone-cold killer. She would do anything for him, but she also understood that she would never be his woman. So she enjoyed the dick whenever he chose to give it, which wasn't often. It really didn't matter to her, just as long as she had a part of him for herself.

"Now listen to me," Lorenzo said as he continued to caress her ass. "Shawty gone be running scared right now but she's not gonna leave the city. You'll get another shot at it but this time I need you to bring her to me," he said with a straight face.

Carmen looked at him with a confused look on her face. Kidnapping was something she had never done before. It had always been just a simple as a bullet to the head then on to the next. That's one of the reasons why she got away with so many murders.

"So you want me to bring her to you alive?" Carmen asked, not really sure about breaking her own protocol.

"Yeah I got something I wanna ask her before I personally put a bullet in her head," he said.

"But how am I supposed..."

"Look C, I don't need you to ask any questions. I

just need you to take care of that for me," he said, cutting her off.

Carmen looked down at the seriousness in his eyes and knew if that's what Lorenzo wanted it wasn't to be questioned. She smiled, leaned in and kissed him again.

"Say no more."

Lorenzo knew that Carmen's kiss was her way of trying to reassure him that she would deliver on his request, but he wasn't worried. Between Carmen and the other hit man he'd hired, Lorenzo had no doubt that Alexus would be brought to him. He was also waiting on information regarding Lala's whereabouts. After testifying she had vanished. The only reason Lorenzo hadn't put a hit on her life was because although she was responsible for getting him locked up she was also responsible for getting his murder charge dropped. More importantly, he did love Tania. Lorenzo had already murdered her father; he decided to give greater consideration before doing the same to her mother.

★

"Brittani girl, I'm so glad you were able to come visit me today. I have so much on my mind and I needed to be around somebody that knows Dior, the good the bad and the ugly."

"That would definitely be me. We go way back to our Philly days. What got you stressing now? Wait…wait…wait…before we get into that, I have to ask, did you get the part?"

Dior sat there with a sad look on her face just messing around with Brittani. It was a brief moment of silence before Dior busted out in laughter.

"Hellll yeah I got the part," she said, jumping up from the bed.

"Aaaaahhhhh!" Brittani screamed, jumping up and hugging Dior. "I'm so proud of you."

"Thanks girl! I needed this, but it's also part of the reason I'm stressed."

"I'm not following you."

"Now that I'm about to make a comeback I have to talk to Lorenzo. He can't find out I'm really alive by seeing my face across his television screen."

"You ain't lyin'. The good thing is, he's locked up. So if he does find out before you have a chance to tell him yourself, at least he's in jail so he can't kill you." Brittani caught the frown on Dior's face. "It was a joke!"

"Don't joke like that. Plus I hate that Lorenzo will probably spend the rest of his life in jail. I would do anything for him to get out. Even if he's locked up I want him to hear the truth from me. But maybe I really should just fade into a life of obscurity. It would be a lot easier than having to explain myself to Lorenzo."

Chapter 13

Lorenzo pulled up in front of the 40/40 Club in his black Bugatti Coupe, turning every head that was standing outside. He was in all black everything, shittin' on niggas without even trying. When he made his entry into the jammed-packed club, the only person with him was his henchman. There were nothing but beautiful women everywhere, but not one of them would be leaving with Lorenzo tonight. Only moments earlier Lorenzo had Precious escorted inside and she was waiting for him in the V.I.P. She was his unofficial date for the night.

Once Lorenzo made it to the V.I.P. section, his eyes lit up when he saw Precious sitting there already drinking a glass of champagne. Even with all the other gorgeous women in the club, Precious stood out like a superstar because she not only exuded beauty but impeccable style and class. Her plunging yellow silk Diane Von Furstenberg jumpsuit clenched her body like it was her second skin. It was complete with ruffle detailing and a Chanel chain belt that highlighted her tiny waist.

"Happy Birthday," Precious beamed, putting her champagne down and giving Lorenzo a hug.

"You really are the best present tonight. You look absolutely beautiful. Thank you for coming."

"Of course I came. I wouldn't have missed your birthday party."

Lorenzo and Precious had developed an extremely close relationship over the last few months, but he when he invited her to come to his birthday party he wasn't sure she would come. He could sense some reluctance and he understood why. Although her husband Supreme had been spending the majority of his time in LA while Precious stayed in New York, they were still married. Lorenzo knew he had to be cautious and not push her too hard. But when Lorenzo wanted something he pursued it relentlessly, and Precious was on his radar heavy.

Phenomenon took the stage and shut it down with a couple of his hit singles before dropping a new, never-before-heard song from his upcoming album. The crowd went crazy. He had everybody in the club hyped.

Lorenzo and Precious scooted out of the V.I.P. booth, walking through the heavy crowd as security moved people out of their way, until they made it up to the stage where Phenomenon was waiting. Then, the music shut off and the whole club looked up at the stage.

"YO, I WANNA GIVE A SPECIAL SHOUT-OUT TO MY RIGHT HAND MAN AND BUSINESS PARTNER, LORENZO," Phenomenon yelled into the microphone. "WITHOUT HIM I WOULDN'T BE

HERE RIGHT NOW. I LOVE YOU MY NIGGA. HAPPY BIRTHDAY!!" he shouted, clapping with the microphone in his hand.

Phenomenon then passed the mic to Lorenzo who stood there for a moment and took in all the love he was receiving from the crowd.

"YO, I JUST WANNA SAY WE A TEAM AND WE EATIN' OVER HERE. SO IF YOU WIT' US WE GOT PLENTY TO SHARE...TO SHOW YOU WHAT I'M TALKIN' 'BOUT, CONSIDER ME THE FIRST NIGGA TO MAKE IT RAIN A HALF MILLION IN THE CLUB," Lorenzo said pointing to the ceiling.

Precious couldn't help but smile at Lorenzo's announcement. He made her think back to when Supreme was a superstar rapper and how hard they used to party together. It was somewhat nostalgic to her thinking how quickly things can change.

When he did that the lights started flickering and out of the sky fell 10 and 20 dollar bills. The club went bananas. Phenomenon jumped back on the mic and began hitting another song from his album called "Money Mayhem." Everybody was dancing and catching money from the sky at the same time. One of the many things Lorenzo had mastered was how to throw an unforgettable party. He hadn't had this much fun in a very long time and it made him reflect on the first time he noticed Dior in a club when she was with Sway. Lorenzo knew from the moment he laid eyes on her that she would be his. Now Dior was gone, but Lorenzo felt he finally might have a second shot at love with Precious.

★

Dior sat alone, poolside trying to put her life in perspective. It was late, so most of the residents at Rockview were asleep. The peacefulness made it the perfect time to relax by the pool and gather her thoughts.

Dior sat there kicking her feet in the water, thinking about the progress she had made and how much she had changed as a person over the last several months. She felt more mature and responsible now that she'd left the cocaine and pills alone. Dior had received a swift reality check on how her life could have been if she continued down the path she was heading. It was the fame Dior had been chasing all this time, but in all actuality she realized that she was going about it the wrong way. She'd spent so much time standing in other people's shadows like Sway Stone and Lorenzo; she'd hardly made a name for herself. She took the relationship with Sway as a valuable lesson to never depend on a man to do for you what you can do for yourself.

Lorenzo, on the other hand, was a good man for the most part, and the love of her life. But no matter how much Dior loved him, she always felt like it was one-sided and she didn't have all of his heart, or even deserve it. Then the day Lorenzo was arrested and Lala showed up telling her all about their relationship was a major blow. Lala made her believe that Lorenzo was really in love with her and that she was nothing more than a charity case for him. That fucked Dior's whole head up. Dior never told Lorenzo how his betrayal completely broke her heart. With Lorenzo in jail and believing he wasn't in love with her the way she was with him, at that moment she really had wanted to die.

"I see I'm not the only one who comes down here at night to think," Erick said as he walked into the pool area.

"Hey, I thought you'd be out tonight," Dior responded, glancing over at Erick who was dressed like he was going to a party.

"I was out but it's hard to have fun when you're constantly thinking about somebody else," he said, kicking off his Gucci loafers. He hiked his linen pants up a little then sat right next to Dior, sticking his feet in the water.

"I'm surprised you even want to be this close to me after what happened between us."

"I can't lie, I was angry, but it's my fault."

"Why do you say that?"

"First and foremost, I'm your sponsor. You came here with some serious addictions. Through our sessions I knew you were fighting some pretty powerful demons. I shouldn't have pushed you so hard but I started falling in love with you and that clouded my judgment. I made a mistake and I owe you an apology."

"Erick, I played a role too. It wasn't like I pushed you away. Honestly, I enjoyed the attention from you. You made me feel special again."

"Dior, you are special. I think that's one of your biggest problems. You don't recognize how special you are. I think once you do it will help build your self-esteem."

"You're right. I do have to work on building my self-esteem. Being in this program has helped me tremendously, but I definitely have more work to do."

"I think this part you got will help. Getting back to work will be good for you."

"Erick, I wanted to talk to you about that. I might have to pass on the part."

"What…why? I went out of my way to make that happen for you because I thought that's what you wanted."

"I know, and I appreciate it, I really do. But I have to clear things up with Lorenzo before I get myself out there. I mean, he thinks that I'm dead."

Erick shook his head in dismay. "You must really love this man."

"Yes, I do. After graduation and I get myself settled I'm going to make contact so I can visit him in jail. I need to explain to Lorenzo in person why I made him believe I was dead."

"I tell you what. Handle that situation and when you're ready the part will be waiting for you. If not this role then I'll make sure you get another one"

"You would do that for me?"

"Dior, I believe in you, so yes."

"Thank you from the bottom of my heart. I mean that."

"I know you do. So have you started packing your things yet?" Erick asked.

"Yeah, I started. I still can't believe it's really over. This place has become like my home and I'm scared to leave."

"That's a natural, healthy fear but you're ready. If I didn't believe that I would have you stay longer. Know that you're not alone in this. I'm still your sponsor and your friend. Whatever you need to make the transition from Rockview to normal everyday life back in the city, I got you."

Dior was thankful that after all was said and done Erick still had her back. She needed all the support she could get as she began this new chapter in her life. The first few months would be the most difficult and having Erick as an ally boosted her spirits.

***

"Close your eyes," Lorenzo directed Precious, as she sat on the sofa in Lorenzo's living room.

"I must've never told you that I hate surprises."

"I thought all women love surprises."

"I can't lie, that is true. Let me rephrase what I said. I love the actual surprise. but the build up to getting the surprise in my hand is what I hate."

"I have a remedy, I won't make you wait long. Open your eyes."

Precious's mouth dropped when she opened her eyes and was greeted with Harry Winston. "Lorenzo, these are for me?" she said in an astounded voice, gasping over the Lily Cluster diamond drop earrings. There appeared to be over eighty brilliant diamonds in a platinum setting.

"You're the only beautiful woman named Precious in here, so yes, they're for you. Put them on."

"They're absolutely amazing, but I can't take these from you. I don't even want to ask you how much they cost. This is way too much."

"So you can't take a gift from me because of how much it costs? It's just money."

"It's more than that. It's what it symbolizes."

"Yes, it symbolizes how close we've become in the last few months. You're very important to me. I consider you a friend."

"Lorenzo, we are a lot more than friends. We see each other at least three or four times a week."

"True, but during all that time we shared together we've never crossed the line."

"Maybe not physically, but mentally we did months ago."

"So what's stopping us?" Lorenzo said, as he sat down next to Precious and caressed the side of her face. His gentle touch sent flutters through her body that seemed to have been balled up yearning to be released. Lorenzo leaned in with ease and placed a light kiss on her lips. They were even softer than he had imagined.

"I can't do this. I'm a married woman," Precious said, pulling away.

"Yeah, in name only," Lorenzo refuted, before leaning back in and kissing Precious again. She pulled away once again. Lorenzo didn't say another word; instead he raised his hand up and placed it on Precious's waist, pulling her body up to his. His other hand reached up and grabbed the back of her neck and pulled her in to meet his lips. This time Precious didn't resist. She couldn't resist his touch. Her body melted into his, and before Precious knew it, she wrapped her arms around him and returned his kisses.

The body of a woman that Lorenzo loved felt so good to him. Since getting out of jail he had fucked, but being with Precious he knew he was about to make love. Lorenzo led Precious upstairs to his bedroom.

He stood staring at Precious for a moment before they undressed each other. Lorenzo then pulled her closer to him, kissing her lips, her neck and right down the center of her chest. He scooped Precious off of her feet, pressing her down on the bed. She wrapped her legs around his waist and her arms around his neck and gasped in pleasure as his dick entered her soft warm flesh.

"Sssssss! Lorenzo," she moaned as he pushed every inch of himself into her. "Yessss," she whispered in his ear as she sprinkled kisses over his mouth and neck.

Lorenzo kept going deeper until completely filling her insides. Precious' pussy was tight and wet like she hadn't had sex in months. He kept stroking and pushing himself deeper inside of her.

"Oh gosh, I'm cumming!" Precious purred in pleasure, trying to hold on to the bedpost for support. Lorenzo could feel her pussy tighten up around his dick and it was like a warm light shower when she came all over his dick. Their kisses became more intense and passionate as they both moaned in pleasure and their bodies shook. Lorenzo was trying to hold back but he couldn't. Her pussy was too good and the way she looked as she was cumming brought Lorenzo to his peak.

"Damn baby, you feel so good," he said as he stroked harder.

"So do you," Precious moaned grabbing a hold of his back.

Lorenzo stroked and stroked and stroked, until Precious came again at the exact same time as Lorenzo. His body went weak as his dick was still rock hard, throbbing inside of her. "I can't get enough of you," Lorenzo said in a low tone, rubbing the tip of his nose up and down Precious's slender neck.

"I can't get enough of you either."

"I'm glad you feel that way," Lorenzo kissed Precious before they began making love again.

Chapter 14

Alexus parked on 123rd and walked over a block to one of her stash houses. She kept a few grand there for instances like this where she need to skate out of town in a hurry. She felt like her run in New York was up and the best thing for her to do at this point was to leave before she ended up dead.

The first thing Alexus did when she got into the house was to grab a bottle of Ciroc out of the cabinet and then head for the living room. She turned the radio on and began dancing to the music on her way over to the couch. If this was going to be her last day in the city she was going to throw a little private going away party for herself, and only inviting herself.

"Throw it up, Throw it up, watch it all fall down," she sang along with Rihanna.

She pushed the couch over with one hand while holding the Ciroc bottle in the other. The carpet that the couch sat on was pulled up and a latch was lifted so that she could reach in the floorboard and grab the money she had wrapped in a Ziploc bag along with some powder cocaine.

"Still go my money!" she continued to sing to the music.

She put everything back, walked around and took a seat on the couch, tossing the money on the table. She continued drinking straight from the bottle, taking large gulps at a time. It didn't take her long to bust open the bag and retrieve the cocaine from it. It was only a couple of ounces but it was more than enough for her solo party. She hit line after line then chased it with the Ciroc. The room was spinning within seconds causing Alexus to fall back on the couch. She was high as hell.

"Bitch, you better not move a fuckin' inch," a voice said from behind, somewhat getting Alexus' attention.

Alexus thought that the cocaine had her tripping out and hearing voices. Then she felt the cold steel pressing up against the top of her head. She tried to look up but everything was blurry. Carmen kept her gun pointed at Alexus as she walked around to the front of the couch. Alexus' eyes started to adjust and when they finally did all she could do is think, "Fuck". She looked up at Carmen only waiting for the blast that would end her life, but it didn't come.

"What are you waiting for? Pull the fuckin' trigger," Alexus spit. "Do it. Do it, bitch!" she blasted, only to get no response from Carmen. "Ohhh, I know what's going on. Lorenzo wants you to bring me to him," Alexus smiled, seeing that Carmen wasn't trying to pull the trigger.

Carmen reached into her back pocket and pulled

out a pair of zip-ties and threw them at Alexus.

"Put these on," she demanded, but Alexus looked at her like she was crazy.

"Bitch, I'm not puttin' shit on. I'm not goin' nowhere. If you think I'ma let you take me back to him, you dumb as a bag of rocks, sweetheart. The only way I'm leavin' this house is in a body bag," Alexus said, leaning over and sticking her nose in the cocaine and sniffing.

Just as Alexus was bringing her head up from the table, Carmen swung the compact black .45 automatic right at her face. Crackkkk!

The side of the gun hit Alexus right at the top of her nose breaking it instantly. She fell backwards on the couch and was knocked out cold. Blood ran from her nose like a river. Carmen tucked her gun in her back waist, walked over and zip-tied Alexus herself. She tapped her on the side of her face to wake her up but Alexus wasn't budging. The cocaine mixed with the alcohol had her comatose.

"Shit!" Carmen yelled to herself, frustrated that she went unconscious from one blow.

There was no way in hell Carmen was going to move her like this. The continuous flowing of blood had also turned Alexus' white shirt red. So even if Alexus was to wake up, she couldn't walk the streets like this without drawing attention. Carmen was going to have to wait it out, at least until Alexus woke up and the sun went down some. Until then, Carmen grabbed the Ciroc bottle off the table and joined the party.

"You did it, Dior. I'm proud of you," Erick leaned over and told Dior while she sat amongst other graduates in Rockview's Ballroom.

Everything was finally going good in Dior's life right now. She was drug free, her career would soon be back on and she had a good friend in Erick who understood her dreams and aspirations. There wasn't any pressure from anybody, nor was there any drama in her life. Sitting here imagining what was in her future made Dior happy, a feeling she hadn't felt in a very long time.

"Dior, can I speak to you for a second in private?" Brittani asked in a panicky voice when she came back from the bathroom with a newspaper in her hand. Dior got up from the table, excusing herself from Erick. They walked over to the bathroom and went inside.

"You're not gonna believe who's in the newspaper today," Brittani said, smacking Dior in the chest with it.

"Phenomenon hosted a birthday party, so what?" Dior said, shrugging her shoulders, looking down at the large photo.

"Look a little closer, Dior," Brittani said, poking at the newspaper with her finger.

Dior took another good look at the paper and gasped at the sight of Lorenzo standing on the stage next to Phenomenon with a huge bottle of Ace in his hand. The photo was taken right at the moment the money fell from the ceiling, so it looked crazy nice. But then it felt like somebody had sucker punched Dior in the stomach. There was a woman standing right next to Lorenzo with her arms around his waist and a big smile on her face.

"When in the hell did he get out of jail?" Dior asked, unable to take her eyes off the photo.

"Girl, I don't know. Ain't you happy your boo home?" Brittani said with a hint of sarcasm.

"I guess there's no need for me to go visit him in jail. He's home and clearly celebrating," Dior seethed, balling the newspaper up.

"Calm down. I know you're upset seeing him with that woman, but in Lorenzo's defense he does think you're dead."

"Yeah and obviously he's replaced me already." Dior couldn't put into words how crushed she was. Lorenzo looked so happy in the pic as if she was the furthest thought from his mind.

"Listen Dior, I'm sure this is painful, but that's why I told you before to do you. Yeah it's fucked up that Lorenzo thinks you're dead, but it hasn't stopped him from living his life, and you need to do the same."

Dior looked over at Erick, "You're right, Brittani. It's time for me to live my life. I'm not delaying shit. I will take that role. I have another opportunity to be rich and famous. This time I won't fuck it up," Dior promised herself.

*****

After many months of searching, the man he had hired to locate Lala had finally come through. It seemed she had vanished without a trace, but if you hire the right person and pay enough money, anybody can be found. Once Lorenzo got the information, he caught a flight and then drove to a quaint house located in Durham, North Carolina. It was on a charming, tree-lined street, the perfect place for a mother to raise her young daughter.

Lala looked out the window and her heart dropped when she saw Lorenzo walking towards her front door. She was panic-stricken and didn't know what to do. She no longer carried a gun. Once she left New York and moved to Durham, Lala thought her days of carrying a weapon were behind her. Now danger was knocking at her front door and she felt helpless.

At first Lala ignored the knock on the door hoping that Lorenzo would go away, but she knew that was unlikely. Her car was parked out front and she needed to leave shortly anyway to pick up Tania from her daycare. The knocking continued and Lala wondered if Lorenzo could hear her heart beating through the door.

"Lala, I know you're in there. I saw you peeping through the curtains when I was walking up." Lala put her head down feeling defeated. The only thing that gave her a flicker of hope was that she didn't hear anger in Lorenzo's voice. Maybe since so many months had passed his hatred for her had simmered down.

Lala unlocked the door and slowly opened it, praying the entire time that she wouldn't be greeted looking down the barrel of a gun. "Lorenzo, please don't hurt me. Tania doesn't have her father. Please don't take away her mother."

"Are you gonna let me in?" Lala stepped to the side and Lorenzo came inside.

"Your home is beautiful," Lorenzo remarked,

observing the expensive furniture, paintings and décor in the spacious home. "What, you win the lottery, Lala?"

"Something like that."

"Yeah, I'm sure you did."

"I know you didn't come all this way to see my home."

"You know why I'm here."

"Lorenzo, after my testimony got you out of jail, I was hoping all could be forgiven and the slate could be wiped clean."

"It's not that easy."

"Alexus manipulated me. She swore to me that you killed Darell. I was hurt. But now I know it was all lies and it was actually her."

"Why would you say that?"

Lala had somewhat prepared herself in case this day ever came. She hoped her revelation would free her from this dark cloud hovering over her, once and for all. "Follow me. I have something I want you to read."

Lorenzo followed Lala into the kitchen and she opened one of the counter drawers. She pulled out an envelope and handed it to Lorenzo.

"What's this?"

"Just read it." Lorenzo opened the envelope and began reading the letter that was inside.

Dear Lala,

Baby if you find this letter, which I know you will, I'm probably dead by now. The first thing I wanna tell you is that I love you and

Tania so much! You are my world, the both of you, and my family was all I lived for. I tried to be the best man and father that I could be, and for the record, I never during the whole time we've been together cheated on you. You was perfect in every way so there was no need for me to look elsewhere. You know you got dat wet wet! lol...

Also I wanna thank you for blessing me with the most beautiful daughter in the world. She's my one and only Princess and I thank God for allowing you to deliver her to me. She reminds me of you so much. She's pretty, goofy, loving and she has a smile that lights up the room. I have to say, you did one hell of a job.

Now, because I don't have a lot of time, I have to get straight to the business. As you can see, it's a little over three million dollars in this safe. Most of it is Lorenzo's and I need you to get it to him ASAP. He was dealing wit a chick named Alexus and she was stealing from him like crazy, but she wasn't the only one. She had a couple more people in our crew working wit her. They were taking Lorenzo's coke money, buying product from somebody named Sosa on the other side of town and putting it back out on the block before he noticed anything.

You know Lorenzo is my boy. I got mad

love for him, so when I found out what was going on I took matters into my own hands. One day I followed Alexus to her stash house off of 129th street. Anyway, I ran down on her, took her in the house and forced her to give me every dime she had. She broke down the operation to me offering me a chance to get in on it. My loyalty was with Lorenzo so I turned it down. Da bitch tried to kill me in that house but I got away with the money.

Now I'm sitting in our kitchen writing you this letter because I know that it's about to be a war. It's kind of late and I tried to call Lorenzo and put him up on everything that was going on but he's not answering. I don't want dat bitch and her crew to run in here for this money so I gotta go to them. I'm locking all the money up in the safe right now. Two million belongs to Lorenzo. That's what I took from Alexus. The rest of the money is mine, well yours now.

In closing, I want you to take care of yourself and our daughter and always know that I'm looking down on y'all. Tell Lorenzo I got mad love for him. He's a good dude and I know he's gonna look out for y'all while I'm gone. Let me get out of here.

Love you,
Darell...

"He used your birthday as the combination to open the safe," Lala said, breaking the silence once Lorenzo had finished reading the letter. "Thank goodness for Tania. She was the one who reminded me your birthday was the day after Darell's. So you know I still have your money. I didn't spend one cent of it." Lala said, walking over to a safe she had in a hallway closet. "When I figured out the combination all I wanted to do was get out of town and start my life over far away from all the bad memories and hell in New York. I wasn't sure who would try to kill me first, you or Alexus so I took Tania and ran."

"Damn," was all Lorenzo could say at first. Everything Darell wrote in the letter made sense. Deep down inside Lorenzo always felt that killing Darell was the wrong move. It was funny how Brice and a couple more people from his crew had said that Darell was stealing money. They had beaten Darell up so bad before he was brought to him that the only thing Darell could do was plead for his life.

The whole time money was coming up missing it was Alexus who was the one taking it. Darell was only trying to expose her, but instead had the tables turned against him. Only to then be killed by the one person he was looking out for. Alexus and Brice knew that Lorenzo wasn't going to ask too many questions when it came down to somebody stealing from him and they definitely knew that their word was going to hold more weight than Darell's.

Lala walked over with the bag and placed it on the floor next to Lorenzo. "Based off this letter I'm positive it was Alexus who killed Darell. I'm so sorry Lorenzo that I ever believed that you would take Tania's father from her. You deserve to hate me because I am responsible for you spending time in jail and for hurting the woman that you loved. I heard about Dior's suicide. I'm sure you partly blame me for that too." Lala swallowed hard as guilt flooded her.

Lorenzo stood there in silence. He was starting to feel the shame of killing an innocent man, taking him away from his girl and his daughter. It was crazy because Darell was his friend. It was evident from the letter that his loyalty was with Lorenzo. Lorenzo couldn't help but feel utter contempt for allowing Alexus to manipulate him like this.

"Darell didn't deserve...he didn't deserve to go out like that," Lorenzo said as his own guilt got the best of him. Part of Lorenzo wanted to tell Lala that he was the one who killed Darell, but then he realized that no matter how he tried to justify it, Lala would never understand. She was from the hood but she still didn't understand the streets. "Just take good care of my goddaughter. Let her know that her Uncle Lorenzo loves her very much," Lorenzo said, walking towards the door.

"Wait, what about the money?" Lala asked, trying to hand him the bag.

"Put that money up. It's yours now. What do I look like taking the money that Darell died for? You put that money up and take care of Tania with it. I'm sure that's what her dad would want."

"Lorenzo, wait," Lala called out, running back

to retrieve something else from the kitchen drawer. "Tania wanted you to have this," Lala said, walking up to Lorenzo while he stood at the front door. It was your birthday gift. She was so disappointed when we left town and she couldn't give it to you herself." Lorenzo stared at the drawing and almost choked up.

"Tell Tania that I love it and I will always love her."

"I will."

"And, Lala?"

"Yes?"

"All is forgiven." Lorenzo now felt responsible for the safety and well being of Lala and Tania. From this point on they were his family. "I give you my word that I'm going to be here for you and Tania forever, no matter what. I'm only a phone call and a flight away." Lala watched Lorenzo walk away speechless. All she could think was Darell's letter had saved her life. Even in death, he was making sure that she and Tania were protected. For the first time since Lala and Lorenzo fell out she believed there was a real possibility that maybe they could get back together and finally be a family. Darell and Dior were both dead and there was nothing and no one standing in their way. Tania loved Lorenzo and Lala thought that if Darell had his choice, he would want Lorenzo to be her man and raise his daughter as his own. Lala believed if she played her cards right, she would make it happen.

Chapter 15

Lorenzo sat in the office of the private investigator that he had hired to check out Dior's death and the funeral Courtney said she had for her. When the guy walked back into his office he had a blue envelope stuffed with papers. He tossed it on his desk and took a seat in his chair.

"Well, I got some good news and some bad news," Ralph said, kicking his feet up on the desk.

"Just cut the shit and tell me what you found," Lorenzo demanded, eyeing the frail white man sitting there looking like he had all the power in the world. His attitude quickly changed once he saw Lorenzo wasn't in the mood to entertain his bullshit.

"There isn't a death certificate for this woman Dior you asked about. Which means that she is still alive out there somewhere or her body hasn't been recovered yet. I'm guessing that she's still out there though."

"Why you say that?" Lorenzo asked, sitting up in his chair to make sure he'd heard Ralph correctly.

"Well, I went to the cemetery and I found out that the whole funeral was a fake. The woman Courtney only recently purchased that plot and tombstone for a few hundred dollars," he explained.

Lorenzo sat there in disbelief as he allowed his brain to process everything he had just heard. To think that Dior might not be dead was fucking with his psyche. Part of him felt a sense of optimism learning that the woman he was still very much in love with might be alive, but then the devil started tapping on the left side of his shoulder.

Dior really didn't love you. She was lying the whole time just so you could help her become famous. Once she got her name out there she didn't need you anymore. She was happy you went to jail so she could run around free. She ran off with another nigga. She's in love with somebody else. She's fucking and sucking on his dick. She hates you. She probably helped get you locked up. This crazy bitch wanted to get away from you so bad, she faked her own death.

All these thoughts ran through Lorenzo's mind in a matter of minutes. The devil definitely was getting the best of him. He felt so sick, so betrayed, so disrespected. If what the investigator was telling Lorenzo was true and Dior was very much alive, the game had completely changed. Instead of her being the woman he was in love with, Dior had become his enemy.

Lorenzo's cell phone started ringing as soon as he walked out of the private investigator's office. He looked down at his phone and saw that it was Carmen.

"Tell me that you took care of that," Lorenzo answered in a frustrated tone.

"Yes, baby, it's taken care of," Carmen responded, looking over at a groggy, but well awoken Alexus sitting up on the couch. "I do got a small problem though. I need you to come to me boo. I can't come outside right now cause the baby is sick," she spoke in code.

Lorenzo understood that to mean something had happened and more than likely Alexus was injured to the point where Carmen couldn't move her. If that was so, it was putting a kink in Lorenzo's plans. Right now, his brain was on one thing and one thing only, and that was to find out where in the hell Dior was.

"Look, I'm taking care of something right now. I'm not gonna be able to get around to seeing you for at least the next couple of hours. You think the baby will be alright until I get there?" Lorenzo asked, walking up to his car.

Carmen looked over at Alexus, whose nose had stopped bleeding for the most part. She then looked over at the bottle of Ciroc on the table along with the cocaine that was spread out next to the bottle.

"Yea, she should be alright. I have some medication here that should knock the pain right out," Carmen smiled.

Lorenzo hung up, confident that Alexus was secured. The news about Dior had his mind so warped he was tempted to tell Carmen to kill Alexus and be done with it. But Lorenzo's hatred against her was personal, and that meant if Alexus was going to die, it was going to be done by him and him alone.

★

Dior's phone ringing nonstop woke her up. She peeked over at the clock with one eye open to see that it said 3:30 a.m. She let it go to voicemail, but as soon as she was about to nod back off, the phone began ringing again. She reached over and grabbed it from the nightstand and answered it with an attitude.

"What?" she said, rolling over onto her back.

"Yo wake up. You keep talkin' like you wanna be a star. Well stars get up in the middle of the night and take long flights to the other side of the country to do interviews and attend private parties," Erick said into the phone.

"Erick?" she asked, still trying to listen to his voice to make sure that it was him.

"Who you think it is, Dior? Our flight leaves in two hours. Wake up, get dressed and be..."

"Flight? What do you mean flight? Where are we going?" She was now sitting up in the bed.

"I hope you didn't think that we were filming in New York. We're going to Cali, baby. So get up, get dressed and be out front in one hour," Erick said, before a moment of silence took over the phone. "Yo, why you still on the phone?" he snapped at her.

"Okay! Okay! I'm getting up now," Dior said as she jumped out of the bed and headed for the bathroom. She knew Erick was testing her. He could've given her some notice about the flight but she figured he purposely waited until the last minute to see how badly she wanted this life. When Dior told Erick that her situation with Lorenzo had been dealt with and she wouldn't need to delay taking the role he was thrilled, but also skeptical. So if Dior needed to prove to Erick how much she wanted this life, she had no problem doing so.

Erick was about his business. He had all kinds of events lined up for Dior to help her gain some much-needed exposure. It wasn't easy making a name for yourself in the world of television. Erick had to not only get Dior's face seen in Hollywood but also by the men and women that owned it.

Dior walked outside at exactly 4:45 a.m. where she got into an awaiting car that took her to a small, private airport in upstate New York. She hadn't been in her apartment in Manhattan for 48 hours and she was already leaving it behind. She looked at all the flashing lights of the city one last time before she got on the highway.

Once she arrived to the airport she was driven to a hangar where several G-4 and G-5 jets sat idle. Watching Erick step down off the G-5 made reality set in quick.

"Yo, let's go," Erick said clapping his hands as he walked up to the taxi. "We don't got all day."

Dior had never seen Erick in this element before, but it was kind of cute, even though he was rushing her. He was in his zone. He knew how to separate business from his personal life and he did it very well.

Dior got comfortable on the jet. It had spacious seating and 19-inch flat screen televisions dropping from the ceiling. It had a mini bar, an optional fold out dinner table and one personal flight attendant.

Erick smiled and sat in the seat right across from her. He reached over, grabbed her hand and cupped it into his. This was the Erick that Dior knew who made her feel warm and secure. He kissed her hand, then looked her in the eyes.

"Everything will be fine, Dior," he said reassuringly. Erick made her feel safe and that's all she really needed.

Lorenzo waited patiently for Courtney to finish shooting Phenomenon's music video before he confronted her about Dior. He knew they were almost finished and he wanted to make sure business was handled first, just in case he ended up breaking Courtney's neck.

"Damn, cuz, you a'ight over here?" Phenomenon asked, seeing Lorenzo off in a daze.

"I'm good. Just have some heavy shit on my mind. Let me ask you a question. If I told you that I thought Dior was still alive, would you think I was trippin?"

"Hell nah brah. I don't put the Makaveli past anybody. Why you think she's still out there?" Phenomenon asked seriously.

"It's a possibility, son. I'm in the process of tryna find that out now," he said, as he looked over at Courtney standing in the midst of several females.

Phenomenon shook his head. He wanted to chill and kick it with Lorenzo but the producers were calling him to get the video wrapped up. He looked out to what he considered some average-looking chicks with a couple of exceptions, standing around waiting to shake their asses.

"Shit, I hope Dior is still alive 'cause I'm in desperate need of some sex appeal up in dis joint," Phenomenon chuckled as he got up and walked off onto the set.

Lorenzo had to agree. There weren't too may chicks in the game right now that could bring life to a video like Dior could. Almost any rapper would choose having Dior by herself in their video as opposed to having five to ten other video vixens. But none of that shit really mattered to Lorenzo. Dior always meant more to him than some piece of eye candy. That's why he had to find out once and for all if she was dead or alive.

When they finally finished shooting the video, Lorenzo was waiting patiently as Courtney walked off the set.

"I see you did ya thing out there," Lorenzo commented when Courtney walked up. Courtney was pretty, and she had a crazy body, just a little rough around the edges. She was by far the baddest chick on the set, and if given some time and proper grooming, she probably could become the next big thing in the music video game. The only thing that stood in her way right now was Lorenzo, and depending on how she handled herself, her career may be short lived.

"How about I take you out for dinner? I know you must be hungry," Lorenzo offered in a polite way.

"Hell yeah, I'm hungry. Let me just grab my things," Courtney said, walking away to get dressed.

Courtney had been in the industry long enough to know not to turn down an invitation, especially from somebody as important as Lorenzo. She had it in her mind that she was going to take full advantage of the opportunity in hopes that he would help her move further in her career.

"So where you taking me?" Courtney asked, flipping the sun visor down to check herself out in the mirror.

"Shit, you the star, you tell me where you want me to take you," Lorenzo responded, only making small talk to keep Courtney's mind off of being aware of her surroundings. It was working, too. Courtney was so caught up in her "I have a dream of being famous speech," she didn't even notice how the scenery outside had changed from being in a highly populated area to riding down streets where everybody was ghost. It wasn't completely dark outside but the sun was about a half hour from disappearing into the night. In that time, Courtney would soon find out her fate also. Because if she didn't fully comply and do precisely what Lorenzo demanded of her, Courtney would also be disappearing into the night, just like the sun.

Chapter 16

After the long flight from New York to California, the first thing Dior needed was a nap. She was jetlagged and her stomach was tossing and turning all over the place.

"You damn right we gone be there tonight," Erick said, coming out of the bathroom.

His voice woke Dior up but she wasn't quite yet ready to get out of the bed. She rolled over to see him standing by the window with a pair of sweatpants on and no shirt. His whole body was cut up so the muscles in his back moved with every hand motion he made as he talked on the phone.

Dior mustered up the strength to get out of the bed and walk over to the window where he was at. He didn't even jump when she wrapped her arms around him and kissed the back of his shoulder. He just kept talking on the phone like it wasn't nothing.

"Aright, I'll see you tonight then," Erick said before hanging up the phone. "Yo, you got a party to attend and a walkthrough at Greystone Manor tonight," he said, turning around and giving Dior a kiss on her forehead.

She reached up and met his lips with hers while her arms rested around his neck. She looked out of the window for the first time since she'd been in the hotel room. The view of Hollywood was beautiful. It looked like one big expensive playground.

"Damn, I love you baby," Dior blurted out.

Erick looked down at her strangely, wondering if he had just heard what he heard. By the time Dior realized what she had said it was too late to take it back or try to clean it up. She had gotten caught up in the moment and only said how her heart felt at the time. She did love Erick. It wasn't the same sort of love she had for Lorenzo, but it was the exact sort of love she needed right now in her life.

"How do you know?" he asked. "How do you know that you love me, Dior?"

She sat there and looked at him for a moment, not sure as to what to say. She had never really thought about it until now, but the more she looked into his eyes, the more she began to realize why she felt that way.

"Because you make me a better person. With you I feel good about myself. I know you want what's best for me and no matter what you have my back. How can I not help but love you?"

"What about Lorenzo?"

"I told you, that situation has been handled. Lorenzo has moved on with his life and I want to move on with mine with you because I do love you."

"Do you love me enough to move in with me when we get back home?" he asked with a smile on his face.

"Damn, I've only been in my apartment for one day," she snapped at first, but quickly caught herself. "But if that's what you really want, then yes, I will move in with you, baby," she said as she threw her arms back around his neck and kissed him.

He grabbed Dior by the waist, and even through the fluffy cotton bathrobe, Erick could feel her thickness. She could see the lust in his eyes and encouraged him to take what he wanted by pulling the strap on the robe and opening it so that he could see what he now possessed. Erick could never get tired of seeing her body, nor could he resist it when she put it on display the way that she did.

He backed her up to the bed with endless kisses, wrapping his arm around her back and gently laying her down on the bed. After taking off his sweatpants, Erick stood for a second enamored with her beauty. His patience had paid off and all of Dior finally belonged to him. Erick leaned over, never breaking eye contact with her, and then kissed Dior's soft lips. He interlocked his fingers with hers pressing them down on the bed over the top of her head. She gasped at the pleasure he gave her, opening her legs a little wider so that he could put all of it inside of her wetness.

Once every inch was in, he let it sit there deep within her womb. Erick took it slowly, wanting to learn every intricate detail about her body. Today he was going to make love to Dior. "I love you too," he whispered into her ear as he slowly slid his dick out before pushing it back in even deeper.

★

Lorenzo pulled over on a dark, empty narrow rode off the highway. Courtney looked around outside to see nothing but trees and grassland. There wasn't a house or a building in sight, nor was there any traffic. She looked over at Lorenzo, willing to do anything. Courtney had no problem giving him some pussy, especially if it was going to help her get ahead.

"What are you up to, Lorenzo?" Courtney asked with a grin on her face letting him know she was down for whatever.

Lorenzo didn't have a smile on his face though. He opened the center console and wrapped his hand around the butt of 9mm, pulling it out and sitting it on his lap. The atmosphere in the car changed drastically after that. Courtney realized that she wasn't there for a sex rendezvous.

"Where's Dior, Courtney?" Lorenzo asked, turning to look out the window. "Now before you answer that question, I want you to understand that this will be your only chance to tell me the truth. If you lie to me I'ma shoot you just to wound you. Then I'ma make you get out of my car and walk in these coyote-infested woods," he threatened.

Courtney didn't even have to think twice about it. She began having diarrhea of the mouth, telling everything that had transpired after he had gotten locked up. She told him about Dior wanting to start her life over without him or Sway being a part of it, about the fake funeral and how Dior paid her to do it. Courtney even offered to repay Lorenzo the money he gave her for the fake funeral that never happened. She also explained that Dior went to rehab to kick her cocaine addiction. Even though Courtney didn't know the location of the treatment center, she gave him the name.

Courtney cried during her confession, hoping and praying that he wouldn't kill her, or even worse, leave her to be eaten alive in the coyote-infested woods. Dior was cool and all, but in Courtney's eyes she wasn't worth dying for.

"Here's what's gonna happen. I own you. Any video you do for Phenomenon is free from here on out and when you do videos for anybody else, you make sure you give me every dime until I'm paid in full. Only then are we done. Do you understand, Courtney?" Lorenzo asked in a calm, yet frightening voice.

Courtney nodded her head in agreement as she wiped the tears from her face. She had stopped crying but she was still scared to death. The whole ride home she stayed quiet as a church mouse, only thankful that she was still alive.

The Kanye West song "Flashing Lights" was blaring in the club when Dior and Erick came through the door. That song was truly a classic, but after all this time it still made Dior feel a certain type of way whenever she heard it.

"The club is crazy packed tonight," Dior yelled over the music. "I can't wait for us to get to V.I.P. so we can sit down," she said as she walked beside Erick.

"Oh yeah, I knew I forgot to mention this while we were out shopping today," Erick yelled back.

"Mention what?" Dior asked, stopping Erick in his tracks in the middle of the dance floor. "It ain't no V.I.P. jumpin' tonight for you," he said. "Tonight is all work and no play. You gonna be workin' the floor tonight," he said, as he waved to a couple of people that he knew.

Erick had major plans for Dior. He wanted everybody that was somebody to recognize her face and name. The same way Dior had dreams, so did Erick. He had already made more money than he could ever spend, so making more didn't motivate him. He had always wanted to take a virtual nobody and create a superstar. That was Erick's plan for Dior and he wouldn't stop until he turned his dream into a reality.

Chapter 17

Lorenzo pulled up, parked in front of the bodega and waited for Carmen to come out, which she did in a matter of seconds. She looked up and down the street before getting into the car. Lorenzo could tell that she had an attitude and it all came from the fact that she had to babysit Alexus for the past couple of days, which she hated to have to do.

"I know you mad at me but I'ma make it up to you," Lorenzo promised before she could even get out a word.

That still didn't stop Carmen from voicing her opinion. "I don't kidnap people Lorenzo. That's not my thing. And how the fuck did a couple hours turn into three days. You got me babysittin' while you off doing whatever da fuck you was doin'," Carmen snapped.

"Alright, alright, Carmen, damn," Lorenzo said, reaching in between his seat and grabbing the yellow envelope full of money.

"I don't want ya damn money...wait, yes I do. Give

me that damn envelope and come get dis bitch out of my house," Carmen went off.

"You got her in ya crib?" Lorenzo asked in shock.

"Yeah, and dat bitch smell," she popped. Lorenzo started laughing at Carmen. She punched him in his arm hard, but playfully.

"Come on ma, let's go take care of this," Lorenzo said, putting the car in drive and pulling out of the parking spot.

They drove all the way to Carmen's house, talking and laughing about stuff they used to do in the past together. He softened Carmen right back up, but not as much as he thought he would. "And you not killing this bitch in my house either," Carmen said as they pulled up into her driveway.

"Come on C. Where da hell else I'ma do it? "I'll muffle the sound so your neighbors won't hear shit," Lorenzo pleaded as they walked up the steps to her house.

"I'm not cleaning up her blood. Plus, I'm not helping you clean it, nor am I helping you drag her corpse out of here either," Carmen responded, sticking her keys into the door.

"I got you. I'll get the cleanup crew here as soon as I'm done."

"Back up Boozer!" Carmen yelled at her pit bull who was trying to push his way out of the door.

"Yeah put dat crazy ass dog in the backyard before I put a bullet in his head," Lorenzo threatened.

After Carmen let the dog out she headed straight upstairs with Lorenzo following behind her. "What da hell," Carmen said, noticing that the door to the back room was open. She got to the room, then turned and slapped the door out of frustration seeing that Alexus was gone.

"Where da fuck is she?" Lorenzo yelled out, looking into the empty room.

"I don't know. I had dis bitch hogtied with zip ties where she couldn't move her hands or feet," Carmen said.

Lorenzo walked into the room and saw the zip-ties on the floor. He picked up a couple of them then looked around the room to see how Alexus could have gotten them off. The room was pretty much empty and there wasn't anything sharp enough to cut it, which made Lorenzo look back at the zip-ties.

"I don't believe dis shit," he said giving the zip-ties a closer inspection. "She had your dog chew through them," he said, giving Carmen the zip-ties before walking out of the room.

He was really regretting not letting Carmen just kill Alexus when she had the chance. He knew that at this point it was going to be hard, if not impossible trying to find Alexus again being as though she had escaped death. The only thing that Lorenzo had to his advantage was the fact that Alexus didn't have any money. She would have to creep through the city on a very low radar until she came up on enough cash to skate out of town.

"I really can get use to this," Dior told Erick as she

was walking back to the car with shopping bags galore. Beverly Hills was one of the most expensive places to shop in America, and Dior was having a ball making it her new best friend.

"Well you need to get used to it, 'cause this is gonna be your new life from here on out," Erick said, standing by the trunk while Dior put her stuff in. "I need you to listen to me Dior. From here on out there's no going backwards. Those hood dreams are over. You Hollywood now," he said with authority.

"Yeah, but I can't forget where I came from Erick."

"And I don't want you to. The hood prepared me to be the person that I am right now but at the same time I know how being on some hood shit can destroy you out here. We're dealing with whites and Jews who run this business and only care about one thing and that's money. If you're not making them no money then they don't have no need for you," Erick schooled.

He had to put Dior up on how things work in the filming industry. It was a completely different world where urban magazines were considered to be amongst the bottom feeders in the eyes of multi-million dollar producers.

"You know, that's why I love and respect you," Dior said, slamming the trunk of the car. "I can always depend on you to keep it 100 with me," she said, wrapping her arms around his neck.

Erick looked around nervously, seeing if any paparazzi were around. Dior realized what she was doing and quickly removed her arms from around his neck.

"I told you, when we out in public this shit is

strictly business, baby. Trust me, you'll see in the long run what I'm talking about," he said, walking her around to the passenger side and opening the door for her.

That was one thing Dior didn't understand. She wanted to show her affection towards Erick to not just Hollywood but to the world. She appreciated all that he had done for her, and being affectionate was Dior's way of showing it. The thing was, and what Erick was well aware of, is that it was too early in the game for people to see that Dior was in a serious relationship. Beautiful, single women in the movie business seemed to get more attention than the women that were married and dragged their husband or boyfriend around with them all the time.

Selling sex was even more prevalent in Hollywood than in the hood industry. The only difference is, the amount of zeroes going across a woman's bank statement after they used what they got to get what they want. If a producer or a CEO or a writer thinks that he has a chance of sticking his dick into a rising star, that woman is more likely to get a role in a movie before the women that is married. And if she doesn't get the role, she's definitely going to be on the radar.

That was the nature of the beast in this business and Erick was going to make sure Dior explored every opportunity that was presented to her, even if he had to sacrifice public affection for a while. Erick's mission was to make Dior a superstar, and knowing the potential that she had, it was going to be well worth it once she really got on.

Chapter 18

"Damn! Who in the world is that?" Phil asked, seeing a woman getting off the elevator looking sexy as ever.

"Oh, that's Melanie, the new chick, she works in records," Jake answered as if the woman walking by them didn't ooze sex.

Melanie walked onto the 4th floor strutting in a tan and white blazer with nothing but a white laced bra underneath, a white knee length skirt and some tan Jimmy Choo pumps. Even in office wear her body was still ridiculously stacked and her natural beauty only added to the package. The woman had heads turning as she passed by the cubicles on her way down to the executive office. The sight from the back was just as good as the one from the front.

C.E.O. Jermaine Knox watched from his glass office as Melanie approached with nothing less than an attitude on her face.

"Look, I'm going to have to call you back,"

Jermaine told the person he was conferencing with via telephone.

"Mr. Knox!" Melanie greeted when she entered his office with a couple of folders in her hand.

She slammed the folders on his desk then walked over and began closing the blinds so that the people outside the office couldn't see what was going on. Jermaine couldn't keep his eyes off of her ass while she turned the little stick that shut the blinds.

"If you give me a minute I can explain, Melanie," Jermaine began to plead, knowing he had messed up.

Melanie walked over to him, unbuttoned her blazer, hiked her skirt up a little then straddled him while he sat in the chair. Jermaine could see her nipples through the lace bra when she raised and rested her hands at the top of his chair. She leaned in and began kissing Jermaine slowly, but very passionately while he reached up and rested his hands on her ass. As hard as he tried not to, Jermaine couldn't help it. His dick began to rise and for the fourth time, Dior could feel it too.

"CUT!" Dior yelled out to the producer as she jumped up from the chair. At this point she was already tired of playing the role of Melanie and she had just started. "Y'all gotta get him some type of cup or something cause he can't stop his dick from getting hard every time I straddle him," Dior said in frustration, walking over and taking a seat in her chair.

The producer along with one of the cameramen sympathized with the young actor. Hell, there were times when their dicks got hard watching Dior act out certain scenes. She had that sex appeal and was able to pull off the raunchy attitude the show needed, and even though Dior made the show better the producers really couldn't afford to keep wasting time and money on unnecessary cuts every time she felt uncomfortable.

"Listen, Dior. You can't keep stopping in the middle of scenes," Erick told her as he walked up and stood next to her chair.

"I know, but the only dick I want rising up on me is yours. It's bad enough I got to kiss him. It feels like I'm cheating on you right in front of your face," she responded.

"Fuck that, Dior. As long as his dick not goin' up in you, I can care less. At the start of the day when you walk into this studio, you're an actor, and at the end of the day when we're laid up in the bed, you're my woman," he explained, hoping it would build her confidence. His words of comfort didn't go very far because Dior didn't feel any better about it, but for Erick, she was willing to deal with it and get the scene done.

"A'ight Tony, I'm ready," Dior said, jumping up and heading back on the set with a new attitude.

The producers didn't know what Erick said to Dior but whatever it was they were pleased that it worked. She got back on the set and knocked the scene out with no problem. It turned out great too. Better than what everybody expected. Dior was definitely on the verge of making a name for herself in Hollywood and as long as she continued to produce the way she had been, more doors were going to open up for her. The kind of doors

Dior had only dreamed about.

★★★

"Lorenzo, you know your relationship with Precious is putting me in a fucked up situation with Nico. The three of us are supposed to be running our business together but he doesn't even want to be in the same room with you," Genesis explained while the two men had dinner at Megu.

"I know the last several months hasn't been the ideal situation for anybody. So much has transpired, but Precious has decided to fall back from the relationship."

"I had no idea. When did this happen?"

"Recently. Remember I told you about Dior."

"Yes, your ex that committed suicide."

"Turns out she's not dead at all."

"I'm not following you."

"Some shit wasn't adding up so I hired a private investigator. Precious found out about it. I had never discussed my relationship with Dior and Precious thought I needed to figure my shit out before we went any further in our relationship."

"Did you figure it out?"

"Somewhat. Dior is alive but I haven't had the opportunity to confront her about all of her lies. I've been trying to resolve a lot of other unnecessary bullshit but it keeps piling up. Honestly, I think it's for the best."

"Why do you say that?"

"Genesis, I believe if I saw Dior right now, I would

kill her with my bare hands. That's how much I hate her for putting me through this."

"You mean that's how much you love her."

"You always been such a wise nigga. If it weren't for your love of the streets, illegal activity and criminal history, you could've been the President of the United States. That's how smart you are." Both men laughed.

"Luckily I'm not, because if I was I wouldn't have time to sit with you and analyze your love life."

"True indeed. So, wise man, what do I do?"

"Whatever you do, don't kill her. Can you promise me that?"

"I've learned in life that promises aren't meant to be made, only broken."

***

Club Martini threw a premier party for the entire cast of Baller Chicks. Dior's role was small but she was invited too because she had made such an impact on the show. Dior's great impression with other actors and the crew hadn't gone unnoticed. It was rumored that they planned on offering her a much bigger role if she agreed to sign on for the next season.

"Damn this place is crazy," Dior yelled over the music to Erick when they took their seats in the V.I.P. booth.

Before Erick could even order drinks for his team, four bottles of champagne were brought over to the table by the waitress. Dior looked at Erick who shrugged his shoulders.

"Compliments of the owner," the female waitress said before walking away from the table.

"Ohhh my goodness! Can I steal her for a minute, Erick?" one of the main characters on the show asked as she and another actress stumbled over to the table.

They both looked a little tipsy but at the same time it looked like they were enjoying themselves.

"Come on Erick, she's all right with me," Sherrie said, grabbing a hold of Dior's arm and pulling at her.

Erick gave Dior the nod letting her know that it was cool, even though Dior didn't feel comfortable. They pulled Dior straight out to the dance floor where she was forced to shake her ass a little. After a while it started to become fun and before you knew it, Dior and Sherrie had a crowd of people surrounding them.

Both of the girls were pulled away by Bianca, another star from the show, and taken over to the bar.

"Girl, you rocked it today," Bianca yelled.

"I know, we gotta try and get you to stay on the show," Sherrie cut in, waving for the bartender to bring them some drinks.

The bartender brought over three shot glasses and a bottle of Tequila. Bianca grabbed the bottle poured some in all three glasses and sat the bottle down.

"I don't drink," Dior said, shaking her head at the shot glasses.

"Come on girl, it's our day. We celebrating tonight," Sherrie insisted, grabbing Dior's glass and handing it to her.

"It's only one drink," Bianca chimed in, raising her glass.

Dior thought about it. She'd been clean and sober from drugs and alcohol for months now. Tonight was a special moment in Dior's career and one drink wouldn't hurt, she reasoned. She had landed a role in a major television show. If that wasn't a call for celebration, Dior didn't know what was.

She took the shot glass from Sherrie and raised it in the air. They all toasted to the Baller Chicks show and threw their drinks back. It burned like hell going down Dior's throat. She had to beat on her chest from the way it fell. After the first one, shot after shot after shot were given to Dior, who threw them back while she went back to grinding on the dance floor.

"She's gonna have a crazy headache in the morning," Dave said to Erick as they watched Dior from the V.I.P. "You think we should go get her?" Dave asked.

"Nah, it's cool. Let her enjoy herself tonight. She's been working hard lately. Did you talk to Eddie about setting up that meeting?" he asked Dave, turning around to face him.

Even when it looked like Erick was partying, he was still at work. Eddie was a producer that worked for Tyler Perry, and was looking for some new talent for an HBO series they were about to start. Eddie and Erick were somewhat cool. They did a few projects on some low budget films a while back and made out pretty well. Just recently before all of that, Eddie was hired by Tyler Perry to work on one of his movies. From that point on,

Eddie was the man and Erick was trying to cut in on him with Dior.

"Yeah, we got the meeting with him but he told me that it was like 200 girls auditioning for the part," Dave said, grabbing the champagne and taking a swig.

"I'm not worried about those other broads. Once they get a taste of Dior, it's a wrap," Erick said with confidence, as he turned to look back out at the dance floor. "Where the hell did Dior go?" Erick asked, throwing up his hands.

"I don't know. Do you want me to go find her?" Dave asked.

"Nah, it's cool. She'll be alright for now," Erick responded. "Now tell me about the HBO series they got boiling..."

"Girl this shit just like old times," Dior laughed, as she along with Sherrie and Bianca stumbled into the bathroom.

They all were drunk as hell, but for Bianca and Sherrie the party had just started.

"We gotta introduce you to Max so you can be a permanent cast member," Bianca said.

"Who in the hell is Max?" Dior asked, barely able to keep her composure from being so tipsy.

"Max is over everybody. He own everybody, including the studio we're filming in right now," Sherrie added. "He can make it happen for you. All he want is one thing," she said, pushing her tits up and laughing.

"I gotta throw up now," Dior turned and headed for the stall.

Everything she had ate for dinner was now floating in the toilet. The whole bathroom was spinning when she stepped back out. Her eyes adjusted on Bianca and Sherrie who were over by the sink. As Dior was walking by, Bianca was snorting a line of cocaine off the sink. Going in right behind her Sherrie snorted the second line. She threw her head back so her nose wouldn't drip. It was a familiar routine Dior was aware of.

"Hit a line. It'll even you right out," Bianca said, passing her the rolled up 100 dollar bill.

Dior didn't even hesitate. It was like second nature to her once she had the liquor in her system. She took the bill, leaned down, put it in her nose and sniffed. The rush was like doing it for the very first time. She went straight to Fantasy Island. She wiped her nose off then looked into the mirror at her dilated pupils that became fuzzy all of a sudden.

Dior was so high she didn't even hear the bathroom door open, nor did she see Erick walk in. He looked at Dior, who still had the rolled up bill in her hand and a little residue of cocaine on her nose. She finally turned around to see him standing there and before she could say anything he snapped.

"What the fuck is you doin' in here Dior!" Erick roared, snatching the bill out of her hand and throwing it at her head.

Bianca and Sherrie scurried out of the bathroom, not wanting to get in the middle of the altercation. They didn't know Dior well enough to put their careers on the line for her.

"What the fuck did I do wrong?" he said, grabbing her face and mushing her cheeks together. "Tell me Dior. What did I do wrong?" he yelled, pushing her up against the wall.

Dior was so high she couldn't even respond to him. The cocaine took over her brain and had her in stuck mode. "This what you want! You wanna go back to being a fuckin' junky. Huh, is that what you want?" he continued to bawl.

Erick couldn't contain his anger and knocked the shit out of Dior. He hit her so hard that it actually brought down her high somewhat because she began to speak.

"I'm sorry, baby," she cried, now realizing what she had done. "I didn't mean to," she continued trying to walk up to him.

The more she sobered up the more she cried and begged for Erick's forgiveness. Erick was furious, but he could see the regret in Dior's eyes. His anger turned into sympathy and he could no longer take her crying. He put his hand on the back of her neck and puller her close to him. He damn near wanted to cry too.

"Yo, we gone get through this, you hear me," he whispered in her ear. "I promise you we're gonna get through it," he assured her and then walked her out of the bathroom in his arms.

Chapter 19

Dior woke up with a splitting headache. She slowly sat up in the bed and looked around the room. A cup of water and a pack of Alka Seltzer sat on the nightstand next to the bed. Erick left it there 'cause he knew she was going to need it after last night.

"Erick!" Dior yelled out as she reached over and dropped the Alka Seltzer in the cup.

He didn't answer because he wasn't there. Dior got up and walked to the bathroom. While she was flushing the toilet she heard the hotel room door open and close.

"Erick!" she yelled out again.

"Yeah," he answered letting her know that it was him.

After washing her hands, Dior looked at herself in the mirror and took a deep breath, exhaling with her eyes closed. The events that had happened last night flooded her mind all at once. She put her head down in shame just thinking about it.

Dior didn't even want to come out of the bathroom to face Erick, but she knew she couldn't stay in there forever. She walked into the room to find Erick standing by the bed putting clothes in one of the suitcases. Dior walked over to the bed with a confused look on her face. She didn't think they would be leaving LA for a while.

"What's going on?" Dior asked, walking over to the bed. She looked down to see the plane tickets lying on the bed.

"Nothing. We're done here," he responded, closing up one suitcase and putting another one on the bed. "Come on, get your stuff. Our flight leaves in two hours," he told her.

"Babe, if this is about last night, I said I was sorry," Dior said, walking up to stand next to him.

His body language told Dior that he was still mad, but his words tried to hide it. He spoke in a normal tone like leaving was part of the itinerary.

"You did your part. You came, did a hell of a job playing the role, attended some parties and guest appearances and now you got your first check," he said, reaching into his back pocket and passing Dior a white envelope.

She opened it up and looked inside. It was a check for sixty grand. A smile came over her face for a brief moment but went away when she looked up at Erick, who wasn't smiling. Dior knew something was wrong but she didn't want to start any arguments with him so she began to help him pack without prying any further.

★

Carmen officially had a hard on for Alexus. She had escaped death twice on her watch and it wasn't going to happen a third time. Carmen was well aware that Alexus was at a disadvantage and planned on using it in her favor. For one, Alexus had a broken nose, so more than likely she was going eventually seek medical care. Being as though Carmen had Alexus' first and last name she simply called around to every hospital in New York to see if she had checked in somewhere. It took a minute but eventually Carmen found her at the Brooklyn Medical Center. Just to be sure, she asked the nurse who answered the phone whether or not Alexus was being treated for a broken nose and she received confirmation. It was amazing how if you asked just the right question in just the right way, the medical staff shared information they had no right giving over the phone.

Carmen walked into the Medical Center with a blond wig on and a pair of dark colored shades. She sat in the waiting area right outside of the emergency room and jumped on the phone. It took her every bit of an hour to get there so she wanted to make sure Alexus was still in the building. The nurse confirmed that she was.

"Damn miss, can I talk to you for a minute?" a guy asked walking up and taking a seat right next to Carmen.

Carmen turned around and looked at him like he was crazy. She wanted to take the gun out of her bag and smack him clean across his face for being so desperate.

"Are you seriously going to try and crack on me while I'm in a hospital emergency room?" Carmen said with her face twisted up underneath her glasses.

"I didn't know it was a set time and place for me to talk to somebody as beautiful as you. Besides I might...."

"Dude! I'm good. Now can you please leave me alone?" Carmen shot back, cutting him off.

The guy threw both his hands up in the air, got up out of the chair and walked away from Carmen. He did that in the nick of time, because Carmen almost missed Alexus going by. She got up to follow her but a cop was walking out right behind her.

Carmen paused and waited for both of them to exit the hospital. When they did Carmen followed. To her relief, the cop wasn't even with Alexus. He jumped right in his police cruiser that was sitting in front of the door.

Carmen kept her eyes on Alexus though, and watched as she headed for the hospital's parking lot. It was broad daylight, but Carmen didn't care. She was going to blow Alexus' head clean off her shoulders the moment she got the chance.

When Carmen entered the parking lot she pulled the .40 caliber from her bag and then the silencer. As she walked through the parking lot she screwed it onto her gun. It was a convenient situation because Carmen's car was also in the vicinity.

"Ma'am, are you having trouble finding your car?" the hospital security asked, walking behind Carmen.

He didn't see the gun in her hand because her back

was towards him, giving Carmen the opportunity to tuck her weapon away in her bag before turning around.

"I think I parked over here," Carmen said with a fake confused look like she really wasn't sure.

He almost blew Carmen's cover and she was tempted to shoot him just because of that. By the time Carmen turned back around, Alexus was already in her car. There was no way she could kill her without having to kill the security guard too. So Carmen made the smartest choice and got back to her vehicle before Alexus pulled out of the parking lot.

Carmen wasn't going to let Alexus get away this time, but she had to be smart about how she made her moves. Carmen followed behind Alexus keeping a nice distance between them, waiting for the right opportunity to make her move.

Chapter 20

"Yeah, I'm getting the hell out of this city," Alexus spoke, holding her cell phone up to her ear. She was talking to a dude Ray she used to fuck who was a member of Lorenzo's team. He had given her some money to hold her over. She was using it get a one-way bus ticket out of town.

Alexus rented a room and had the best night's sleep she'd had in a long time and was now ready to bounce. She didn't know how or when Lorenzo or his bitch for hire were going to retaliate against her, but Alexus was trying to slip away before either had a chance.

"You can stay here if you want Ray, but eventually Lorenzo is gonna find out that you was stealing from him too, and when he do, he gon' kill yo ass. I guarantee it," Alexus promised, knowing how sick Lorenzo could be and how easy it was for him to kill.

Alexus hung up the phone 'cause she was tired of talking and her bus was about to leave in about an hour. She was going from New York to Atlantic City, then from Atlantic City to Philadelphia where she was going to catch a flight out to the West Coast. She had it all planned out. Alexus had connections on the West Coast that had no ties to Lorenzo. They were going to put her to work. All she had to do was get there.

Alexus zipped up her bag, picked up the 9mm off the bed and put the full clip in it, then cocked a bullet in the head. She took a look at her nose in the mirror while she fixed her hair. Her left eye was still a little swollen from the blow to her nose but a bitch was alive and that's all that mattered to Alexus.

"Once my money start rolling back in, this ain't nothing a little plastic surgery won't fix right up," she mumbled to herself, picking the gun back up and stuffing it inside of her back.

Before Alexus left out of the hotel room she walked over to the window where she had a clear view of the front of the hotel. She looked for anything suspicious, not wanting to get caught slipping. Everything appeared clear to go but she still had to be cautious since the bus station was six blocks away.

Alexus kept her eyes on alert but she didn't have the slightest idea what was lurking in the wing stalking her like she was prey. There was no chance in hell Carmen was going to let her leave this city alive.

The bus driver stood at the front door of the bus collecting ticket stubs from the passengers before they boarded the bus. Alexus got on and went straight to the back and got a window seat. Moments later a small commotion went on outside and then Carmen stepped onto the bus. She walked straight to the back of the bus, pulling the .40 cal. from her waist and took a seat right next to Alexus.

At first, Alexus didn't recognize her because of the wig and glasses, but she came to know exactly who it was when Carmen spoke. "Somebody wants to talk to you," Carmen said, whipping out her phone and tapped on the screen. Alexus could hear the phone ringing and then a man answered. "Make it fast," Carmen said into the phone, passing it over to Alexus.

The bus driver finished letting the rest of the people on the bus before coming onto the bus and looking for Carmen. He had given her until he finished loading the bus to convince her friend to stay, or at least that's what he thought Carmen was doing.

"Hello," Alexus spoke into the phone with humbleness, hoping Lorenzo would spare her life.

"What's good Alexus? I really didn't have much to say except that it was fucked up how you and the rest of my crew played your cards. You manipulated me into killing a good man. Darell was a true friend, the rest of you are some fake fucks," Lorenzo said.

"Lorenzo, I'm sorry. Please don't do this," Alexus begged.

"My only regret is that I'm unable to be there to kill you myself. Goodbye Alexus," Lorenzo said, and then hung up the phone.

Carmen didn't even give her a chance to say another word. She lifted the gun up to Alexus' face and pulled the trigger. The bullets exited the gun and entered her skull through the front. One out of the two bullets exited through the side, splattering brain matter up against the window. Passengers covered their ears and ducked down in the seats. The bus driver jumped back and fell into one of the empty seats scared to death by what he had just witnessed.

Carmen reached over and grabbed her cell phone from Alexus' corpse. She scanned the bus once, looking at all the passengers who had their faces hidden. Then Carmen walked down the aisle and right off the bus like nothing had happened.

The flight back to New York was quiet, except for the small conversations Erick had with Dave and Fats. It was burning Dior up that Erick wasn't saying anything to her. She had admitted to messing up and thought Erick understood, but it was obvious that she was wrong.

"Can I have a word with you?" Dior asked, unbuckling her seatbelt and walking to the back of the jet to the bathroom away from the ears of everybody else.

Erick got up and followed her just to see what she had to say. His mind was pretty much made up concerning what needed to be done at this point.

"What's up Dior?" he said, cramming into the small bathroom with her.

"I guess me apologizing for what happened last night don't mean shit to you," Dior snapped, tired of getting the cold shoulder. "What happened to us getting through this together?"

"Come on Dior, what are you talking about?" he asked in a nonchalant manner, only making Dior even more pissed off. "I really don't have much to say. All I know is that when this plane lands, you're going back to Rockview. End of story," Erick said, letting Dior know it wasn't up for discussion. He then turned around and walked back out of the bathroom.

Dior was so stunned by what Erick said she couldn't even respond. His words actually made her weak at the knees and she had to sit down on the toilet. The tears filled up in her eyes and within seconds began flowing down her face like a stream. She couldn't believe it. Dior couldn't believe that Erick had spoken to her like she was a junkie he'd just found on the streets. Not like the woman whom he had professed his love to and had sex with. He made Dior feel small, a feeling she hadn't felt in a very long time.

<center>★★☆★★</center>

"It's done," Carmen told Lorenzo over the phone as she got in her car.

"Excellent. Now that that's out of the way, I need to holla at you about something important," Lorenzo said, stepping out of the studio.

The more he thought about Dior and the games she and Courtney had played about her death, the more Lorenzo felt betrayed. He had cried for days over Dior's death and went through extreme emotional trauma he never shared with anybody behind loving her so much then losing her. The only comfort he could get now is if Dior really was dead. It was going to be impossible for Lorenzo to go on with his life knowing that she was still out there alive and possibly happy. Lorenzo felt he could never allow his heart to love or trust Dior again, so death was the only answer to his problem.

After finishing his conversation with Carmen and finally coming up with a solution to his Dior problem, Lorenzo placed a phone call.

"Lorenzo, hi," Lala said, answering his call on the first ring. Lorenzo could practically see her smiling through the phone.

"Hey, how are you and Tania?"

"We're good. She misses you though. She was so happy when you called her before she went to sleep the other night."

"Yeah, I'll have to do that more often."

"She's hoping you'll come visit her soon."

"I'm working on it. But maybe you all will be able to visit me soon. That's why I'm calling you. That situation with Alexus has been handled. You all are safe now." Lala knew that must've meant that Alexus was dead.

"Thank you, Lorenzo. I don't know what Tania and I would do without you."

"Well you don't have to worry about that because I'm not going anywhere."

"Do you really want us to come visit you?"

"Definitely. I told you, you all are my family. I'll be in touch and let you know when is a good time."

"Okay, I'll be waiting for your call." When Lala hung up with Lorenzo she jumped up and down and ran upstairs to Tania's room. "Baby, come give mommy a hug," Lala grinned, lifting her daughter off the bed, spinning her around.

"Mommy I like it when you're happy like this," Tania laughed, kissing her mother on the cheek.

"Mommy is so happy because your Uncle Lorenzo is going to be your daddy."

"Really! Does that mean you and Lorenzo are getting married?"

"Yes!"

"When?"

"Soon, baby. We're going to be a happy family like we always wanted," Lala promised, holding her daughter close.

Chapter 21

3 Months Later…

Lorenzo walked in the lounge area where Phenomenon's video shoot was taking place. Courtney and one other girl were sitting in there watching television.

"Hey Lorenzo," Courtney said when he came in. He simply nodded his head before getting a drink out of the refrigerator. "We're on a break right now," Courtney explained, like Lorenzo gave a fuck. He wasn't cool with Courtney but she had been paying his money back, slowly but steadily, so he at least kept it cordial.

"Ohmyfuckingoodness!" Courtney screamed out, causing Lorenzo and the other video girl sitting next to her to pause and stare.

"What is your issue?" the girl asked with confusion. Courtney couldn't take her eyes off the television. That made Lorenzo turn to see what was on the screen that had her acting crazy. Lorenzo couldn't believe his eyes. It was like he had seen a ghost.

"That's Dior and she's on a freakin' VH1 scripted television show. She went from rehab to this. Get the fuck outta here!" Courtney said with excitement.

A knot formed in Lorenzo's stomach. After all this time, Dior still had an effect on him like no other woman ever had. Seeing her on the television screen he couldn't believe that at one point he had planned to have her killed. If it weren't for Genesis, Dior would be dead. He had convinced him to call the hit off on her. Lorenzo let it go and began living his life like Dior really was dead. Lorenzo had been genuinely happy, up until now. Seeing Dior on the television screen changed all of that.

"What's the name of this show?" Lorenzo asked.

"Baller Chicks," Courtney answered, keeping her eyes locked on the screen.

Tony sat in his office going over a movie script when his assistant, Mario, barged into the room. He had a handful of papers and a huge smile on his face.

"You're not gonna believe the ratings on the show," he said, slamming the papers on the desk in front of Tony. "It's VH1's highest ratings ever for a scripted show and everybody wants to know who the new girl is," Mario said, taking a seat on the office couch.

Mario wasn't lying either. Tony could see from the paperwork that the viewers had nearly doubled. Just as many people tuned in to watch the re-run of the show. Tony had a feeling that Dior would make this type of impact.

Before Tony could say anything, the office phone started to ring. Reading the ratings chart and looking at some of the comments made on Twitter, it wasn't a surprise at all that Max was on the other line. "Maxwell, what can I do for you sir?" Tony spoke in a polite and respectful tone.

Max was what everyone would call the "higher ups". He was the boss of everybody in Tony's studio and most of the time when he called it was to do one or two things. It was to fire you or to congratulate you on a job well done. Fortunately for Tony, he wasn't calling to fire him but rather to congratulate him.

"That was a smart move you made bringing in that new girl Dior," Max said while puffing on his cigar. "You would be even smarter if you made her a permanent cast member."

"I know, sir. Actually, I've been working on that all morning. I looked at the stats and I was crunching numbers before I made an offer to bring her onboard," Tony replied. "You know, I have to stay within the show's budget," Tony added, trying to make it look like he was doing his job.

"Well don't worry about her salary. I'll take care of that. All I need you to do is get her back to LA and have her standing in my office by the end of the week," Max said, then hung up the phone in Tony's ear.

For Max to want Dior as a permanent cast member,

it was huge. Usually females would have to practically beg Tony and Max for roles, but Dior was different. The show actually needed her in the hopes that she would continue to boost the ratings. The viewers were going to be expecting to see more of Dior, and if they didn't, more than likely the ratings for the show would start to go down. Neither Tony nor Max was willing to let that happen.

Dior laid poolside, topless, soaking up the last bit of the summer before the fall hit. It was peaceful too. Erick was out taking care of some business at Rockview and the gardener and landscaping crew were off for today, so Dior had the house to herself, or at least that's what she thought.

"Damn, bitch, put some clothes on," Brittani laughed, walking across the lawn with a laptop in her hand.

It was like she came out of nowhere, messing up her mood.

"How did you get in here?" Dior asked, shaking her head at Brittani's crazy ass.

"I picked that little ass lock on the back gate. I knew you were here 'cause I tracked your phone," Brittani smiled. "Are those real?" she teased, playfully poking Dior's left breast. "I don't remember your tits being that big, Dior," Brittani joked. Dior reached over and grabbed her tank top.

"What do you want Brit?" Dior asked, pulling the tank top over her head.

"Shit, I just had to come chill with my celebrity friend. Your name is all over the Internet and your Instagram and Twitter is off the charts," Brittani said, passing Dior the laptop.

When Dior looked at her page the comments she had from her friends were crazy. Everybody was saying how much they liked her on the show. Others talked about fashion and asked what kind of shoes she was wearing on Baller Chicks. Some people asked crazy questions like if she was really dating the actor she was kissing or if she at least slept with him. Dior was amazed at the feedback and comments she was getting.

"I don't understand. How do all these people know about me?" Dior asked, shaking her head.

Brittani tapped on the screen until she found what she was looking for. Once she did, she passed the laptop back to Dior. She looked down to see the show Baller Chicks on the screen and herself stepping into the office and straddling.

"When the hell did this come out?" she asked in shock.

"Girl, it came out yesterday but they played it again today. Bitch, where the hell have you been?"

Dior had been going through so much with Erick as of late, she really wasn't interested in what was on the television or blogs. She hadn't gotten a heads up from the producers nor did Erick let her know. Leave it up to Brittani to be the one to tell her.

"Damn, girl, we gotta go out," Brittani said, standing up and coming out of her jeans and shirt.

"Girl, what in the hell is you doin?" Dior giggled.

"MY GIRL IS A STAR!" Brittani screamed, running down the deck and jumping clean into the swimming pool.

Dior laughed at her but was inspired by her excitement. It made her get up and follow Brittani's lead.

"I'M A STAR!" Dior screamed at the top of her lungs before jumping into the swimming pool too.

***

"I can't believe this shit, homie," Phenomenon said to Lorenzo. "She's definitely a good actor," he joked.

Lorenzo had to admit he didn't know what to think about the return of Dior. Just a few months ago he wanted her dead and was actually paying somebody to see that it got done. Now he was happy that she was alive. Lorenzo's emotions were all over the place.

"Yo, what are you doin' after this?" Lorenzo questioned, looking around the studio. "I need a drink, my nigga."

"Man, we can roll out right now. I laid two tracks today. I can use a drink myself," Phenomenon replied.

As soon as Phenomenon and Lorenzo left the studio paparazzi swarmed them out of nowhere. They almost got shot running up on Lorenzo the way that they did.

"Phenomenon! Phenomenon! Did you know Dior was back on the scene?" a photographer asked as he took pictures. "Is she going to be in another one of your videos!" another man shouted.

"Phenomenon, are you and Dior an item?" another female yelled out with a recorder in her hand. "Is she here?" she asked.

Phenomenon just moved the cameras out of his face and made his way to his car. People really didn't know Lorenzo that well other than his half million-dollar birthday bash. So none of the paparazzi followed him to his car, nor did they take pictures of him. That was the main benefit Lorenzo enjoyed from making all his millions behind the scenes.

"Are you going to the celebrity bash?" a photographer asked before Phenomenon got into his car. "Is Dior gonna be there?" Phenomenon didn't answer either of the questions. He just jumped into his white Aston Martin and pealed off. Lorenzo pealed off right behind him in his Bugatti.

Erick walked into the house to see Dior standing in front of the television in the living room. Her face was glued to the screen but she was well aware of him coming into the house. He walked over to see what she was watching.

"Why didn't you tell me they were airing the show yesterday? And please don't insult me by saying you didn't know," she added.

Erick looked and saw that the show was on. He was silent for a moment. Erick had known, but he didn't think that Dior needed to know at the time.

"We haven't been on the best of speaking terms

lately. I was under the impression we had bigger issues to deal with," he responded, walking away to head to the kitchen.

"So you didn't think making my debut on television was important enough for you to break the communication barrier? You don't seem happy for me, Erick," Dior said, following him into the kitchen.

"Well congratulations, Dior," Erick said, giving her a fake smile before opening the refrigerator door. Dior immediately picked up on Erick's sarcasm.

"So when are you going to call Tony and try to get me a permanent role on the show?" Dior wanted to know.

"I'm not," Erick shot back without a second thought.

"You're not. What do you mean you're not? The blogs are going crazy and I know the people like me on the show. So what's the problem?" she asked with an attitude.

Erick was really trying to avoid having this conversation, but if Dior was ready, so was he.

"You sure you wanna have this discussion right now?" he warned, stopping what he was doing just to face her.

"Yes, I wanna have this discussion right now, 'cause I'm sensing some jealousy coming from over that way," Dior responded, walking around the kitchen's island to stand right in front of him. "Come out wit' it, Erick."

"Jealous of you. Why in the hell would I get jealous of you? See, you must still be high from the coke you sniffed when we was in LA. I'm a fuckin' multi-millionaire already, Dior. You still got a long way to go before you get to where I'm at," Erick reminded her.

"Oh, is that what this is all about? You still mad because I had a minor setback? I told you I was sorry and I haven't even craved that shit since that night. Okay, I fucked up. You gonna hold that against me forever?"

"You might think that I'm trying to hold you back and I don't have your best interest, but I'ma tell you like this. Until you figure out what caused you to slip up and relapse, you're not ready for Hollywood. When I told you to go back to Rockview, it was for a reason. It wasn't to punish you or make you feel like a junkie. I told you that because I love you and I want the best for you," Erick said with sincerity.

Erick knew the dark side of Hollywood. The side people closed their eyes to. He saw careers of famous actors put on hold due to their addictions. Erick had watched cocaine destroy people's lives in a very short span of time and in some cases he even attended funerals behind the vicious drug. He didn't want that kind of life for Dior. When he walked into the bathroom and saw her sniffing cocaine, it broke his heart, and he felt a great deal of responsibility for not realizing she wasn't ready. Erick felt he had showed Dior too much too soon.

"So you really serious about me going back to Rockview?" Dior asked, putting her head down in shame.

"I am, Dior. All you have do is go back for 30 days. You don't have to do all the groups sessions if you don't want to. I'll set you up with Dr. Elizabeth Miller for one-on-one counseling and that's it. You can even do the outpatient treatment," Erick explained.

"So 30 days and then what?"

"In 30 days I'll call Tony and do everything in my power to get you a permanent role on the show," Erick promised.

He lifted her chin up so that she would look him in his eyes. Dior didn't have a clue how much Erick loved her and wanted nothing but the best for her. Right now he was giving her tough love, but it was necessary.

Chapter 22

Pulling back up into Rockview for the first time in months felt weird considering the fact that Dior had recently graduated from the program. She didn't think that it was necessary for her to have to undergo the mental therapy sessions with Dr. Elizabeth Miller, but Erick was adamant so Dior agreed. She wanted to move forward with her relationship with Erick and her promising acting career. That's all Dior was looking forward to.

"Well, well, well. If it ain't my good ole friend Dior," Ms. Ferra said, walking up to Dior's car. "I thought you'd be in Hollywood by now," she smiled.

"Heyyyy Ms. Ferra," Dior waved, getting out of her car. "Now what are you doing here?" Dior inquired, giving Mr. Ferra a suspicious look.

"Child, I just came up here to check up on a friend of mine who admitted herself a few weeks ago. You know how it get the first month of you being in this place," Ms. Ferra chuckled thinking about the detoxing phase. "What about you? Who you creepin' up here to see?"

Dior put her head down in shame. She felt this way every time she thought about what had happened in LA. "You know I can't lie to you, Ms. Ferra. I had a relapse. It only happened one time, but Erick thinks that I should try and find out why it happened," Dior explained. "I really don't wanna be here. Besides, it was a few months ago and I haven't even thought about touching cocaine since."

"Well baby, as bad as that damn boy Erick works my nerves, he's right. Hell, come to think about it, that boy must feel some type of way about you if he's still trying to keep you straight. Truth be told, I didn't think you and he would last this long," she told Dior as they walked side by side out the parking lot.

Dior was about to respond but her cell phone ringing caught her attention. Tony, the producer's name, came across her screen. She excused herself from Ms. Ferra and answered it.

"Hey Tony. How's everything going?"

"Everything's great. I'm calling because I have some good news for you. I tried reaching out to Erick but he wasn't available. But anyway, we are all in agreement that you should have a permanent role on the show. Of course, we have to go over some numbers with you and your team but other than that you're pretty much in," Tony stated.

"Wow Tony, I don't know what to say," Dior smiled.

"Well, say that you'll be on the next flight out here and that would be good enough for me," Tony said, looking up at the calendar and remembering the deadline Max gave him.

Dior stood there thinking about it. She didn't want to give him an answer until she spoke with Erick. "I don't think that I'm going to be able to leave on such a short notice. Plus, I have a couple of things I need to take care of first," Dior told him.

"Well how about this. I know you'll be at the New York Celebrity Bash on Friday, so how about I come out there we can discuss your future in person?" Tony suggested.

Until now Dior hadn't even considered going to the Celebrity Bash coming up. From what she had heard all the New York artists who were rappers, singers athletes and actors was going to be there, representing the city where it all started for them. It was supposed to be crazy.

"I think that's possible. Just give me a call on Thursday letting me know that you're in New York," Dior said, agreeing to meet.

"Sounds good," Tony said before hanging up.

Dior hung up the phone feeling overwhelmed by the offer. She was feeling like everything was starting to come together in her life. The hard work and dedication was paying off. Her only problem now was trying to convince Erick that she didn't need the therapy and that going back to LA immediately was the best thing. Knowing Erick as well as she did, Dior knew that was going to be an uphill battle, but one she was willing to fight.

★★★★★

Lala sat in her rental car, nervous as she could be looking over at the couple of customers coming out of the bodega. She reached under her seat, grabbed the .38 snub and stuffed it into her leather tote then exited the vehicle. Her mind was racing as she looked up and down the street before entering the store.

"Can I help you?" a Spanish guy asked from behind the counter while he was closing the register.

"I'm here to see Carmen. Is she available?" Lala asked in a polite manner, showing no signs of hostility.

"Yeah, hold up. Carmen!" he yelled to the back. A few seconds later, Carmen came out from the back of the store. This was the first time Lala had ever seen her and to the letter she was exactly the way Lorenzo described her. Carmen recognized Lala but was surprised to see her there.

"Yes?" Carmen said with a confused look on her face.

"Is there somewhere we can talk in private?" Lala asked, looking over her shoulder at the cashier then over at a customer that had just walked into the store.

Carmen nodded her head and then led Lala to the back of the store, opening the same door she had come out of. Lala looked around nervously before going through the door. She wasn't sure how this was gonna to play out.

"Take a load off," Carmen said, pulling a chair from under the table. "Do Lorenzo know you here?" she asked, walking over to the deep freezer and pulling out a gallon of lemonade. Lala was shocked to see that she knew who she was.

"No, he doesn't know I'm here and I would ask that you keep it that way. That would be better for both you and me," Lala advised.

"So what's goin' on? What brings you down here? I thought you and your daughter had moved away." Carmen asked, grabbing two cups and taking a seat at the table.

"Yes, we did. But Lorenzo told me Alexus was dead, and when he came to visit us recently he told me I had you to thank for that."

"Did it. I'm surprised Lorenzo shared that information with you."

"He thought I should know, especially since it was retribution on the woman that took my daughter's father from her."

"I understand," Carmen said nodding her head. "I was just doing the job I was hired to do, but I must admit I took great satisfaction in killing Alexus," Carmen smiled. "But I'm sure you didn't come all this way to personally thank me for getting rid of Alexus."

"You're right, I didn't. The real reason why I'm here is because I need your help with something. Lorenzo and I were in a serious relationship at one time, but several unfortunate factors fucked that up. But now we have a chance to be together again and I don't want anything coming between us. I also know you have your own special relationship with Lorenzo."

"Wait, what are you saying?" Carmen asked with a curious look on her face, trying to figure out Lala's angle.

"What I'm saying is that I have no problem with you. But you're a very smart woman and you know that whatever your relationship is with Lorenzo, that's as far as it will ever go. I, on the other hand, Tania and I are his family. We both play our separate roles in his life and we are respectful to one another whenever we do cross paths," Lala said, pretty much blowing Carmen's mind.

"I'm still not understanding why you feel the need to come at me like this."

"Because I have a proposition that I think will be beneficial to both of us, but I wanted to be upfront and lay my cards on the table for you."

"Now you talkin' my language. What's the proposition?" Lala reached into her bag, pulling out a large wad of money.

"It's a half million dollars in that bag. I want to hire you to kill somebody for me."

"Wow," Carmen said, raising both eyebrows. She had made a lot of money from her murdering skills but no client had ever offered Carmen a half a million for a hit.

"Do you know Dior?" Lala asked.

"Bitch!" Carmen responded immediately to hearing her name.

Carmen knew Dior just as well as Lala did and she probably hated her even more. There was a time in Carmen's life where she thought that Lorenzo could possibly see her as more than his sexy murder for hire chick and that they could explore a relationship. But that dream was snatched away when Dior hit the scene. Lorenzo fell for her hard and fast. She had ruined everything and was protected by him.

"Yeah, I know da bitch, but I can't kill her."

"Why?" Lala asked. If this bitch comes back into his life...Well you already know where that leaves us," Lala said, reflecting back to the moment she realized Dior was still alive. She was sitting at home flipping through the channels and stopped when she saw some woman straddling a man. The woman looked eerily familiar. Lala swore to herself that her mind was playing tricks on her because that woman was dead. But to her horror she was wrong. The woman on her screen was indeed Dior and she wasn't dead after all.

Lala's dreams of marriage and babies with Lorenzo came to a screeching halt. She had been too patient for too long to allow Dior to prance her whorish ass back in Lorenzo's life and destroy all her hard work. When she found out the news she discussed it with Lorenzo but he tried to play it off like he was over Dior and wanted nothing to do with her. Lala knew Lorenzo well enough to know it was all lies. No matter how hard he tried to hide it, Lala could see in his eyes that Dior still had her claws penetrating his heart. That's when Lala knew she had to make her move and get rid of the competition once and for all.

"Since we're putting everything on the table, a few months after Lorenzo found out that Dior had faked her death he hired me to kill her. He didn't want to admit it to me but that bitch fucked him up emotionally."

"What happened…why isn't she dead?"

"Lorenzo had a change of heart. He called me a couple days later and cancelled the hit. That means he still has it bad for the triflin' bitch and he would more than likely murder me if he found out I killed her."

"Lorenzo doesn't have to know it was you who did it. You got a half million dollars, Carmen. Be creative."

Carmen had to think about it for a moment. Lorenzo knew her so well that he could pinpoint Carmen's kills from the manner in which the person was murdered. Carmen had a unique way of killing, one being that all of her victims took a headshot straight to the center of the forehead or to the temple. It was unique because she always double tapped when she did it, similar to the training of the Special Forces. If Carmen was going to kill Dior she was going to have to do exactly what Lala told her to do, which was be creative.

"Look, I gotta think about this. Give me a couple of days to figure some stuff out," Carmen said, leaning back in her chair.

Lala nodded her head, reached over and tried to grab the bag of money thinking that Carmen wasn't going to take the job. But right when Lala reached, Carmen pulled the bag closer to her.

"I'll hold on to this. Like I said, I gotta figure some stuff out," she told Lala.

With that said, Lala got up from the table and found her own way out, leaving with an enormous amount of confidence that Dior's hours were numbered.

Chapter 23

"Yo girl, this Celebrity Bash is going to be off the chain," Brittani told Dior as they shopped in Henri Bendel. "Oooh, this look cute," she continued, holding up a printed Stella McCartney frock. "This dress would be everything paired with some sequin pumps."

Dior really didn't say much. She just walked around the store more so browsing than anything. Instead of being happy about the good news she got yesterday from Tony, Dior was stressed out thinking about the argument she and Erick had earlier that morning.

"Girl, you ain't picked up one outfit yet. What's wrong wit' you?" Brittani asked, seeing it written all over her face.

"Nothing. I probably won't be going to the Celebrity Bash tonight," Dior revealed in a disappointing tone.

"Why, what happened? I know that nigga ain't on some hating shit is he?" Brittani fussed. "Don't be letting no nigga steal your shine. You worked too hard for this."

Brittani didn't understand that Erick wasn't hating on Dior but rather trying to make sure that she was ready to deal with everything that came along with being famous. Dior understood Erick's concerns but she really wasn't feeling it and that had caused their heated exchange.

"Dior, sit down," Brittani said, pointing to a bench inside the store. "Now I know when we was growing up I never really had the chance to give you good advice, mainly because I was learning shit from you," Brittani smiled. "But let me tell you this. It's not too many young black girls coming out of the hood getting the opportunity you got right now. I know chicks that would give anything to be in your shoes. Hell, I'm one of them," she chuckled. "I guess what I'm tryna say is that I'm proud of you and I pray that you don't be stupid enough to blow your chances of becoming what you've dreamed about since we were kids."

Dior sat there and listened. She realized that everything Brittani said made sense and there was no telling if this opportunity was going to last very long. When Tony got into town last night he told Dior that she had until after the Celebrity Bash to have her answer as to whether or not she was flying back to LA with him. It was either go back with him or stay behind and risk the chance of someone else taking her spot.

Erick made his position clear this morning. If Dior got on that flight to LA, he was done with her professionally and their relationship was over. Erick had pushed Dior into a corner and she had to choose between fame and love.

Dior walked into the house with a few bags in her hand. Brittani's speech had pumped her right up to go to the Celebrity Bash despite the lecture from Erick. More than anything, Dior wanted to go out and enjoy herself and not think about anything heavy.

"Look, I don't wanna fight with you, Erick, but I'm going to the Celebrity Bash tonight," Dior said, as she walked into the bedroom where Erick sat with his face in his laptop.

Erick didn't turn his head to look at Dior. "Yeah, go ahead and do you babe," he told her calmly.

His lax attitude caught Dior by surprise. She didn't know if Erick was just trying to be smart or if he really didn't give a fuck. "And what's that supposed to mean?"

"Dior, you gone do whatever you wanna do, anyway. I don't have time to be chasing after you right now."

"So why don't you just come with me?" Dior suggested.

"I have to work. You're not the only actor on my roster. I gotta start lookin' out for them too," he added.

"You know what, Erick, do what you gotta do," Dior said, storming out of the room with her bags in her hand.

Erick sat there for a minute thinking that Dior was going to come running back into the room, but she didn't. The only thing he heard was the front door slamming.

"Shit," he mumbled to himself, getting up from the desk. He wasn't trying to hurt Dior's feelings or to make her upset. He really did want the best for her and wanted to be there for her as well, but at the same time he needed for Dior to listen to him. By the time Erick got downstairs and opened the front door Dior was speeding down the street in her car.

★★★

"Lorenzo, thanks again for letting Tania and I stay here with you while we're visiting instead of having us stay in a hotel. And my mom's apartment wasn't ideal."

"I have more than enough space and I'm enjoying having you both here. A child in the house really does liven the place up."

"Yes, Tania is a bundle of joy and she sure does love her Uncle Lorenzo."

"I love her, too. It's easy to love a little girl like Tania. I'm sure your mother is enjoying having her granddaughter with her tonight."

"She is. It's hard for her, us being so far away. Now that Alexus is out of our lives she's really trying to convince me to move back to New York. What do you think?"

"Being around your family is always a good thing and you do have a lot of family here."

"I was thinking the same thing."

"You sure you don't wanna go with me to this Celebrity Bash? I hate to leave you here alone."

"I'm not really up for going out tonight. Why don't

you stay home with me? I can cook you your favorite dinner and we can watch a movie."

"That is a tempting offer and we're going to definitely do that tomorrow, but tonight I have to attend this Celebrity Bash. Phenomenon has to be there so I have to attend. It's business."

Lala was trying her best to keep Lorenzo home via the request of Carmen who had something planned for tonight. She didn't want Lorenzo anywhere around when shit went down so she had asked Lala to try and keep him away from the Celebrity Bash tonight. That was proving to be impossible and Lala knew why. Dior was supposed to be there and Lorenzo wanted to see her. She knew he was only bluffing, inviting her to tag along knowing full well Lala would more than likely turn him down.

"Come on, Lorenzo. I'm sure Phenomenon can do without you for one event," Lala said, trying to give it one last try.

"I'm flattered that you want me to stay here with you, but I really do have to go tonight," Lorenzo said as he fixed his tie. "I'll try to be back early," Lorenzo lied as he walked to the mirror and took one last look at his suit and tie before heading out. Lala sat back on the sofa admiring how good Lorenzo looked in his designer suit. When he wanted to, Lorenzo could take his dress game to a whole other level, and that's exactly what he did tonight. He was casket sharp.

What had Lala boiling on the inside though was that she knew Lorenzo was dressed simply to impress Dior. The only thing giving her solace was that by the end of the night, Carmen was going to make sure this would be Dior's final cut. If Carmen was as good as Lorenzo said she was, this time, Dior wasn't going to have to play the role of being dead.

Chapter 24

A plush ballroom in Midtown was the designated place for the Celebrity Bash. There were nothing but exotic cars pulling up in front of the building where hundreds of people crowded the streets and sidewalks. This was one of the biggest events in New York each year so everybody who was somebody made it a point to attend.

Paparazzi were posted out front of the Ball Room snapping picture as celebrities walked the red carpet before going inside. Phenomenon was on his all-white everything swag, as he pulled up in his white Aston Martin that matched his all white gear. He stepped out looking like the perfect gentlemen.

"Phenomenon! Over here!" a man yelled, then took his photo. "You look good, man!"

"Thank you," Phenomenon said before disappearing into the ballroom.

Anytime it was time to turn up, Lorenzo pulled out the big boy toys, although all his whips were considered big boy; it just depended on what he was in the mood for. Tonight he opted for a cherry red, Lamborghini Murcielago. As soon as the driver side door lifted up, the cameras started flashing. His all-black Tom Ford suit, cherry red tie that was the same color as his whip and the brilliant cut, flashy yet classy diamonds he wore had motherfuckers thinking Lorenzo really was that nigga, and not behind the scenes but in front of the cameras. The paparazzi didn't have a name to place with the impeccable face but they started snapping away because Lorenzo exemplified a boss, strolling down the red carpet.

Groupies were about to break their necks turning their heads and waving their hands trying to get Lorenzo's attention. But he ignored the hoopla, instead walking through the doors like he wasn't an invited guest to the venue but that he owned that bitch.

"Damn, playboy, you in straight Diddy mode I see," Phenomenon said, nodding with approval as he walked up to him.

"You representin' up in here as well," Lorenzo said giving him dap. "This shit is crazy in here. "I think every bad bitch from all over the world came to show out," Lorenzo was convinced, as there were beautiful women in all shapes, sizes and colors every direction you turned.

"Yup, and that is lovely for me. I'm leaving with a minimum of three hos tonight, but ain't none of them having my baby," Phenomenon boasted. Lorenzo found it funny as hell the way Phenomenon embraced that rap star life to the fullest.

"While you over there pussy braggin' I hope you important enough to get us a section," Lorenzo joked, looking around the room.

"Come on my nigga, what I look like?" Phenomenon laughed, pointing across the room to where his spot was reserved.

Brittani and Dior pulled up together in Brittani's Mercedes-Benz SL-550 with the top down. They both jumped out ready to shut shit down. Dior did her necessary styling and profiling for the cameras as she walked the red carpet. She continued playing it up for the Paparazzi as they snapped away.

"Dior! Dior! Can you turn this way?" a photographer yelled out. "Congratulations on your success," he praised, while taking picture after picture before she and Brittani strutted their clean asses right into the building.

Dior made her entrance into the party wearing a dramatic black and white Jenni Kayne jumpsuit with a plunging neckline that highlighted her damn near perfect breasts. She made sure her look was flawless by wearing some bold chartreuse Jimmy Choo heels that you could spot from across the room. Dior pulled her phone from her clutch and immediately started texting Tony to let him know that she was in the building. She wanted to handle her business with Tony before she did any partying. She got a text right back with directions, telling her to come to his V.I.P. booth on the second level.

"Oh hell nah. I'm about to leave, girl!" Dior exclaimed, frowning up her face.

"Why, what's wrong?" Brittani asked looking around the room.

"You see that chick over there," Dior pointed to a female sitting across the room. "She has on my exact same jumpsuit and my Jimmy Choo's. Where they do that at? This ain't no cheap shit neither. My night is ruined."

"Just chill, girl. You not gonna be here that long anyway," Brittani said, downplaying the situation so Dior would calm down.

Dior agreed, knowing that as soon as she finished meeting with Tony she was out the door.

"I'm about to go meet with Tony. Can you stay out of trouble for twenty minutes?" Dior smiled.

"Yea girl, go ahead and take care of your business. I'ma wait for you over at the bar," Brittani replied.

When Dior got to the top of the steps Bianca met her with open arms. "Heyyy Dior," she greeted giving her a hug.

"Hi Bianca. You came down too?" Dior asked.

"Yeah the whole cast of the show is here. Oh and Dior, I'm so sorry about that night in the bathroom. I didn't know..."

"Don't worry about it Bianca. That was my fault. I just got caught up in the moment. But I'm good now," Dior replied, letting her know that there weren't any hard feelings.

Everybody from the show showed Dior lots of love when she got into the V.I.P. section. Bianca was right, all the girls were there. Bianca, Sherrie, Tanya, Carla, and Destiny. Tony was also there with his right hand man, Andres.

"Come sit down next to me, Dior," Tony said, tapping on the open leather seat right next to him. Dior sat down, shading the champagne offered to her by Tony as if it was poison. For Dior that's exactly what it was.

"Hey Tony, it's good to see you."

"It's good to see you too. I'm going to skip the small talk, Dior, and get right to it."

"That works for me."

"Like I told you, we want you on the show permanently for the next season and possibly another, and maybe even after that, if it continues getting picked up. I'ma be straight with you. Our ratings are skyrocketing and we think it's mostly due to your appearance on the show."

"Dior, we got four shows left in this season and I'm willing to pay you top dollar to appear in them. Not only will you get unlimited exposure, you will be a very wealthy girl.

Dior sat there in a daze not believing what she had heard. Tony was willing to give an absurd amount of money to a small-time actor like Dior. She didn't know whether to scream or to give Tony a big, fat, wet kiss.

"Wow, thank you Tony," Dior said, trying to keep her cool.

"Don't thank me yet. There's a catch to this offer," Tony said, grabbing the glass of champagne and sipping it. Dior knew that the offer had to come with a twist. It just sounded too good to be true.

"What's the twist, Tony?" Dior asked.

"The twist is, you have to leave with us by tomorrow. We put production on hold because we wanted to see if you were going to do the show. So if you accept, we are moving forward to get you back to LA and immediately start filming," Tony said.

"Damn, tomorrow, Tony?" Dior said, putting her head down.

"And not a day later... So what's it gonna be?"

Carmen came through shutting the ballroom down on the low-key level. She had on a light blue Diane Von Furstenberg dress and a pair of strappy silver heels. Her long, curly hair dropped down just below her shoulders. She was dressed as if she was there to catch a man, but that was furthest thing from her mind. Carmen actually came dressed to kill.

Dior carefully trotted down the steps in her heels, desperately needing to talk to Brittani. When she got downstairs it looked as though it was more crowded then when she had first gone upstairs. The bar literally looked like it was a mile away.

Dior began cutting through the crowd, bumping into some people and bypassing others. One dude backed up so hard into her she dropped her clutch. She reached down and grabbed it and when she came back up, she froze in her tracks at the sight of Lorenzo standing in front of her. Her heart sank down into her stomach, looking into the eyes of a man she still loved, and had betrayed and left for dead.

"Can't even lie, you look damn good for a dead woman," Lorenzo said.

Dior didn't know what to say or if she should have said anything, for that matter. She still was in disbelief that he was standing there.

"Awww, come on, Dior. You knew this was going to happen one day. I'm sure you got something to say," he smiled.

Dior stood there stuck on stupid. The only feeling that she had was guilt. She was trying to pull her thoughts together to formulate the words to express all her emotions but she was coming up blank.

"I just have one question for you," Lorenzo said, looking her directly in the eyes. "Why would you tell me you love me but then turn around and hurt me the way you did?"

"I do love you, Lorenzo, that was never up for debate," Dior answered quickly. "I'm sorry Lorenzo," she said, putting her head down in shame.

"You know how many nights I cried over you thinking that you were dead? Do you even know how much of your death I carried, feeling like I was partially responsible for you overdosing?"

The tears began to fill up in Dior's eyes thinking about how selfish it was of her to hurt Lorenzo the way that she did when all he ever did was love her.

Standing there in front of her, Lorenzo had these mixed feelings that were making him damn near delirious.

On one hand, Lorenzo wanted to wrap his hands around Dior's neck and strangle the life out of her right there in the middle of the floor. Then the other side that seemed to be growing faster by the second loved and missed her. Maybe it's true what they say; the heart wants what the heart wants.

Carmen watched Lorenzo and Dior closely from a distance, and even in a crowded room there was no denying their chemistry. They were drawn together like magnets and Lala was spot on about the effect Dior had on Lorenzo. Instead of smacking her, beating her to the ground and stomping her out, Lorenzo was standing there in front of Dior with more sympathy for her than anything. Her submissive demeanor along with a few tears softened him right up.

It was when Lorenzo grabbed her hand and walked off towards the V.I.P. that Carmen got amped. Carmen had had her reservations about killing Dior, but not anymore. Dior's death couldn't be prolonged any further.

"I messed up, Lorenzo. I let my insecurities get the best of me. I never meant to hurt you," Dior cried, sitting on the couch wiping the tears from her eyes with a napkin. "So much was going on and I thought you was about to catch a life sentence. I'm not excusing my choices but I just didn't know what else to do."

"But you left me, Dior. I needed you. No matter

what the situation was, you weren't supposed to turn your back on me. I was there for you when you needed me, wasn't I?"

"Yes, you were there for me and everything you're saying is right, but I was lost without you. It was like in a matter of hours I saw you get arrested, that woman Lala told me you were cheating on me with her and I meant nothing to you and then I almost died of an overdose. I was at my lowest point ever and I had no one to carry me through the storm, so I had to get myself some help."

Lorenzo sat there and listened to Dior. He also vented some more about how he felt. It was something Lorenzo needed to get off his chest. Never in his life had his heart been broken like that, so he needed as much clarification as he could get.

"Can you please forgive me, Lorenzo?" Dior begged, reaching over and placing her hand on top of his.

Lorenzo lifted his head up and saw a woman who resembled Carmen standing in the middle of the floor with some guy close up on her. He focused in and looked harder, and he was sure it was Carmen. At first, he ignored her and kept talking to Dior, but things appeared to be getting tense. He was about to make a move, but resolving his feelings with Dior was the only thing that mattered to Lorenzo right now. "Dior, I'm still in love with you," he admitted, thinking if he admitted it out loud, that somehow it would make the pain he'd been carrying disappear.

"Lorenzo I'm still…"

"Hold that thought. I'll be right back," Lorenzo said to Dior, before rushing off to help Carmen, who seemed to be getting manhandled by some guy. Lorenzo normally would never put Carmen in the category of victim but the nigga harassing her was tall and buff. The only thing that could take him down was another man or a weapon. Lorenzo seriously doubted Carmen had her weapon on her, so he was the next best protection.

"I know you wanna touch it," Carmen said seductively to the guy who couldn't help but to palm her ass with both of his hands.

Dude didn't know what he was in for. Carmen picked him randomly for one purpose and that was to get Lorenzo's attention. She knew that it didn't matter who Lorenzo was with or where he was at, if he saw some man blatantly disrespecting Carmen or he thought she was in trouble, he would come to her rescue.

A few minutes before Carmen saw Lorenzo stand up she decided to turn it up another notch, since Lorenzo wasn't paying her no mind. But now that he was heading in her direction, Carmen slammed her foot on the gas pedal going full speed. Lorenzo was walking up from behind her so to add a little fuel to the fire, Carmen gave her decoy some very encouraging words to think about.

"Dis pussy yours tonight," she said, reaching down on the sly grabbing a handful of his dick getting him overly aroused. Her words gassed him right up, as he started grabbing every part of her body aggressively, thinking that she was into that rough sex. He was giving the effect she needed in order to get Lorenzo out of the way. With swiftness, Carmen glanced out the side of her eye determining how close Lorenzo was. When she felt he was close enough, Carmen then flipped the script.

"Leave me the fuck alone," Carmen screamed at the top of her lungs hitting the man viciously as if she was being attacked. I said stop!" she shrieked. It all went down so fast the man didn't know what was happening before it was too late.

"Nigga, is you crazy! Get yo' motherfuckin' hands off her!" Lorenzo shouted, lunging at the man and asking no questions in the process. Lorenzo served the dude, hitting him with a three-piece combination that knocked him backwards. He caught himself before he fell then charged right back at Lorenzo, throwing a few punches of his own. Lorenzo wasn't expecting for the guy to have friends nearby, but he did, and before Lorenzo knew it he was swinging punches at three instead of one.

"Oh, shit!" Phenomenon yelled out, looking across the floor and seeing Lorenzo engaged in a vicious fistfight. Phenomenon and his boys shot across the floor to help Lorenzo, and once they jumped in it, more of his dudes jumped in and it became an outright brawl. Niggas was throwing chairs and bottles of champagne at each other, while others who weren't involved scattered to get out of the way. People rushed towards the front door pushing and yelling, all while getting hit by flying objects.

Carmen backed off of the fight then looked around before reaching under her dress and grabbing the .380 automatic strapped to her right thigh, then grabbing the silencer strapped to her left thigh. Everybody was so busy fighting nobody even noticed what she was doing. She walked over and snatched a towel off the bar and placed it over the top of the gun in her hand, concealing it from potential witnesses.

At this point, Dior had gotten up out of the V.I.P. section and headed for the door like everybody else. She looked around frantically for Brittani while she tried to push through the crowd.

"Brittani!" Dior yelled out, seeing her about fifteen to twenty yards ahead of her. "Brittani!" she yelled out again, getting her attention.

She wasn't the only person's attention Dior had. Carmen looked up and spotted Dior all the way on the other side of the room. She eased her way through the fight, trying to keep her eyes on Dior but also trying to avoid being struck with something or someone's fist.

As she stalked Dior, Carmen came across Lorenzo fighting two men who looked like they were starting to get the upper hand on him. Once she got close enough, Carmen squeezed the trigger, sending a bullet into one of the men's back. It was so loud in the building nobody could hear the gun being discharged. The man's adrenaline was running so high, he didn't even feel it at first, and by the time he did, Carmen was back on the prowl looking for Dior.

"Bingo," Carmen said, seeing the back of Dior's head still pushing through the crowd.

She knew it was her because of her outfit, so she kept her eyes glued the black and white jumpsuit so she wouldn't lose her.

"Yo, these niggas crazy," Dior said, finally catching up to Brittani. "That's it for this bullshit," she yelled, trying to be heard over the commotion.

The closer Carmen got to her the tighter she gripped the gun. She pushed past one female then was knocked off her balance slightly by a man, but Carmen had Dior locked into her sight. She got within ten feet of her, raised the gun while still keeping it concealed under the towel and pulled the trigger. The first bullet hit her in the back. As she fell to her knees Carmen squeezed the trigger again, hitting her in the back of the head. Her body fell face first to the floor and the only thing Carmen could hear as she faded into the crowd was a woman who was standing next to the woman screaming.

Lorenzo finally broke free from the fight and was pushing his way through the crowd when he saw a woman in the middle of the floor kneeling over another woman who was lying in a puddle of blood He couldn't see the girl's face but he knew from the clothes she was wearing that it was Dior. He tried to push his way over to them but the crowd of people stampeding to the front doors made it difficult. It was like swimming against a strong current. He kept trying though, and as soon as it looked like he had an opening, the guy whom he was fighting previously hit him in the back of his head with a full bottle of Ace. "Dior," was the last word he uttered before taking the second blow from the bottle, which knocked him out cold.

Chapter 25

Erick rolled over in his bed and cracked open his eyes to see that Dior hadn't come home last night. First thing in the morning and he was already pissed off. He got up and walked to the bathroom still half asleep, took a piss, then went downstairs to retrieve the morning paper along with his cellphone that he had left on the kitchen counter. He turned the kitchen television on before going out and grabbing the paper off the front lawn.

"In the wake of the Celebrity Bash brawl last night here in Midtown Manhattan, a female with a promising career was killed inside of this ballroom behind me," the anchor said while looking over her shoulder.

Hearing that when he walked into the kitchen Erick walked over to the TV and turned the volume up. The news anchor described some of the events that took place last night, reporting that another man was in critical condition with a gunshot wound to his back and countless other people who were treated for minor cuts and bruises.

"Damn! I told Dior not to go to that bullshit," Erick said to himself as he picked up his phone to call Dior.

When he dialed Dior's number it rang twice before a man answered it. He pulled his head back from the phone and looked at it like it was crazy. Erick wasn't going to say anything and was two seconds away from hanging up when the man yelled into the phone.

"Hello. Is there somebody on the line?" he asked.

"Yeah who the fuck is this and where the fuck is Dior?" Erick snapped.

"Good morning sir, my name is Detective Nelson with the NYPD," the detective said.

"Well why are you answering her phone?" Erick asked, still a little upset.

"Sir, we believe that this phone belongs to a woman that was murdered last night. She didn't have any I.D. on her but this phone was lying near her body," the detective explained.

The detective even gave a description and the woman matched Dior to the T. It crushed Erick's world to hear of Dior's death, so much so that Erick didn't even have the strength to hold up the phone to his ears. His legs were getting weak so he took a seat on one of the barstools, laid his head down on the island and began crying. He was out of it. Words couldn't explain what he was going through. The loss of Dior was a devastating blow, one that would last a lifetime.

★

Lorenzo walked out of the emergency room holding an icepack to the back of his head. He squinted from the bright sunlight once he got outside. Phenomenon was standing there waiting for him with two cups of coffee in his hands. It looked like he had a rough night too.

"How you feel?" Phenomenon asked, passing Lorenzo one of the cups. "Did you need stitches?"

"Nah bro, no stitches, but my head hurt like a mafucka. That nigga could have done anything but hit me in the back of my head with a bottle", Lorenzo semi joked.

A bottle to the back of the head wasn't no joke. If the guy would have hit Lorenzo any harder he could have done some serious damage. Luckily the huge knot on the back of his head was all that came of it, that and a splitting headache.

"Yo what happened to..." Lorenzo began but was cut off by Phenomenon, who already knew what he was going to ask.

"That wasn't her, son," he answered. "I saw Dior last night once I made it out of the ballroom. I think she was wit' another chick," Phenomenon explained.

Lorenzo swore something bad had happened to her after seeing who he thought was Dior laying in a pool of blood, right before he went out from the blow to the head. When he woke up in the ambulance, Dior was all he could think about.

"You think she's still in the city? I didn't get a

chance to finish talking to her because of all the chaos."

Phenomenon could see something in Lorenzo's eyes when he asked that question. He could tell that Dior still had a part of his heart, and even being the gangsta the he was, Lorenzo couldn't hide how he felt.

"You want her back, don't you?" Phenomenon asked with a smirk on his face as he opened doors and got into the car.

Lorenzo tossed the icepack before jumping into the car with him. He thought about what Phenomenon said and there was no denying the fact that he did want Dior back in his life. After all she had put him through, Lorenzo missed her. The hurt from her betrayal had subsided over time and now all he thought about was picking up where they had left off before he went to jail.

"Dog, I'm not gonna lie. I'ma get my woman back," Lorenzo told Phenomenon as he gazed out of the window.

Phenomenon looked over at him and smiled. "That's my nigga."

"That's crazy, 'cause I was really starting to like Lala," he said.

Once Lorenzo made up his mind that he would get Dior back he thought about another woman in his life, Lala. Although he hadn't stepped over that line again with Lala he knew that she was hoping they could give their relationship another try. Maybe if there was no Dior he would consider it. Lala had proven she would step up for him if need be and he would always have love for her based on that. He also loved Tania and both of them were his family. At this point it wasn't no way he could turn his back on them, especially since he was the reason Darell was dead. The guilt of that alone was heavy. But Lorenzo decided it was time for him to sit down with Lala and let her know that getting back together was no longer an option. He would continue to be there for her and Tania but strictly on some platonic shit. Dior was his future and every chick in his life would have to deal.

*****

Lala parked about a block away from the bodega, then reached over and grabbed the .38 snub nose from out of the center console. Retrieving the large, dark tinted sunglasses, Lala got out of the car and headed down the street, after tucking the gun in her back waist. Her palms started to sweat immediately and the realization of what she was planning to do had started to kick in.

"Come on, Lala, you can do it," she mumbled to herself as she made up her mind that she was going to kill Carmen. It only dawned on Lala after she paid Carmen to murder Dior that she could kill two birds with one stone. Once Carmen got rid of Dior, Lala would kill Carmen, leaving only one woman in Lorenzo's life. And only one person alive who knew she was responsible for Dior's death. She didn't like Carmen having that sort of leverage over her.

Instead of going through the front door of the store Lala walked around back and went down a flight of steps to where the basement door was. She tapped on the door lightly hoping Carmen was there. She tapped a little louder when nobody answered. A few moments later, right before Lala was about to walk away, the locks on the door began clicking. Carmen peeked out, only to see Lala standing there. She opened the door fully then stepped to the side so Lala could enter, which she did. Lala was feeling even more nervous than she had before.

"It's done," Carmen said, closing the door then walking past Lala to lead her into the next room.

Once Carmen was in front of her, Lala took the .38 from her back waist and placed it in her bag. She thought about shooting her right then and there but she wanted to make sure nobody else was there with them.

"Are we alone?" Lala asked, looking around the basement that was converted into an apartment.

"Yeah, it's cool to talk. It's people upstairs but they can't hear us," Carmen answered. "Have a seat," she said, pulling out the chair from the kitchen table.

Lala took a seat and placed her bag on the table. She watched as Carmen walked over to the refrigerator and grabbed some eggs and cheese from off one of the shelves, placing them on her kitchen counter by the stove.

"Are you hungry?" Carmen asked, reaching up and getting a frying pan, then turning the TV on that sat on top of the refrigerator.

"Nah, I'm good. I'm not going to be here that long. Lorenzo didn't come home last night. Did you see him at the Celebrity Bash?"

"Yeah, I saw him," Carmen smiled, thinking about how he came to her rescue. "He didn't get in my way at all. But he did get into a scuffle," Carmen said, walking over and taking a seat at the table with Lala.

"A scuffle…over what?"

Carmen was about to say something but stopped when she glanced up at the TV and saw the building where the bash took place at last night. She grabbed the remote control to turn the volume up so she could hear. Lala looked up at the TV as well, listening to the news anchor describe the scene inside of the ballroom.

"The victim who's been identified as Aisha Parker was shot several times, and was pronounced dead on the scene around 12:25 last night. Some might have known her as Melinda Dover, the up-and-coming singer out of Brooklyn, New York who had a promising future in the industry," the news anchor reported.

Lala and Carmen both looked at each other at the same time, knowing that the young lady the anchor was talking about wasn't Dior. Carmen became frustrated immediately and so did Lala. Carmen started to try and explain what might have gone wrong last night but Lala wasn't trying to hear it.

"That's my bad, Lala. I'ma take care of it," Carmen promised, looking back up at the TV.

Lala kept her eyes on Carmen as she began to reach into her bag for the .38. Carmen turned around at Lala's sudden motion to see her reaching in her bag. Carmen locked eyes with Lala and knew she had seen that expression before. It was the look of a woman with murder on her mind.

"I guess if you want something done nowadays,

you gotta do it yourself," Lala said, gripping the .38 and squeezing the trigger from inside of her bag.

The blast from the gun was somewhat muffled but the bullet ripped through the bottom of the leather bag and struck Carmen in her shoulder, spinning her out of the chair. Lala pulled the gun out of the bag then followed up with several more shots, striking Carmen in the back. Carmen tried to make her escape to the other room where she had set her gun on the couch. She almost made it but fell to the floor a couple of feet away. Lala walked over, cautiously aiming the .38 at the back of Carmen's head. Footsteps could be heard upstairs shuffling around.

Lala rolled Carmen over onto her back. She was still alive, but not for long. Carmen looked up at Lala and spoke.

"Why?" she whispered as she held one hand over the bullet wound to her shoulder.

Lala stood directly over her, aimed the gun to the center of her head and answered. "There can only be one," Lala said, before pulling the trigger, sending a bullet directly to the center of Carmen's head.

Lala was about to tuck the gun away and leave, but then she heard the sound of a door opening. She spun around with the .38 in her hand, only to see a little girl, no older than six, standing in the threshold of the bedroom door. Lala froze and her heart dropped into her stomach at the sight of her. One look and she knew exactly who the father was. The little girl was the spitting image of Lorenzo.

"Carmen!" a man's voice yelled out from upstairs

as he tried to open the door.

The commotion snapped Lala out of her gaze with the little girl. As she backed out of the ground level door, the man came barging in from the upstairs door. Lala fired her last shot towards the top of the steps, forcing the man to retreat before he could come down the steps. That gave Lala enough time to shoot out the door, leaving behind a dead mother and her living child. A child who she knew would come back to bite her in the ass one day.

Erick hung up the phone after talking to Ms. Ferra and was headed down to the coroner's office to identify Dior's body. He still was under the impression that she was the one that was killed at the Celebrity Bash last night. After he had gotten off the phone with the detective earlier, he was sure that it was Dior's body they'd found, so he had stopped watching the news for any updates.

On his way out the door, Erick ran into one of the people from his landscaping crew. In his hand was an envelope with Erick's name on it.

"A woman dropped this off about ten minutes ago," the worker said, passing Erick the white envelope.

Erick took it and opened it up to see the contents inside. He could smell Dior's perfume all over it. Inside was a letter that read:

Dear Erick,

By the time you read this letter I will already be on my way to LA. I wanted to say this face to face but the lack of time prevented me from doing so. I guess I first would like to tell you how much I love you. I know that under these circumstances it might be hard to believe, but it's the truth. You came in a time in my life when I needed someone to be there for me. I never thought that I would ever be able to love again but you proved me wrong. During a time when my life was the most difficult and the world seemed to be against me, your love gave me the strength to get through it. I thank you for that and I appreciate the love you have given me. It got me through some tough times and to be honest with you I really don't know where I'd be if it wasn't for you stepping up to the plate and being the man I needed in my life. You will always have a special place in my heart.

Now, getting to the reason why I'm writing you, I wanted to be the one to tell you that I have been offered a permanent role on the show for the remainder of this season and next. I know that you are against the idea being as though I relapsed and you think I may need further treatment, but I couldn't turn down the offer. I weighed the pros and cons already and I truly believe that this is the best move for me. You know for me this is like a dream come true. You might not think that I'm ready but I am. I've learned so much during my many months at Rockview. When I relapsed that time, it only made me stronger and more determined to let that part of my life go. I don't even have a craving for cocaine any longer. I don't even want to drink anymore. From now on I'll be getting high off of life and all of the money I'll be making doing my thing out here.

I can't lie, it would be nice to have your support out here but I know you and once you feel betrayed it's a wrap, no matter who you are. You're mad at me, I know, but I made this choice for me. I just felt like it was time for me to be in control of my own destiny for a change. I hope that one day you will be able to understand that. Well, look babe I have to go. I'm about to board the jet and have to get this letter to Brittani so she can have it to you by tomorrow morning. Know for sure that I love you and I always will. And whenever you come back out to Hollywood, get in touch with me so we can do lunch.

Loving You Always,
Dior

★

Lala pulled into the driveway, put the car in park and just sat there for a moment. Lorenzo's car was there, so she knew he was home. Before having to face him, Lala held her hand out in front of her to see if it was shaking, but it wasn't. She wasn't afraid, nor was she nervous about what had just transpired. The feeling that Lala had was strange to her. She almost felt numb.

"What in the hell did you do?" she mumbled, looking at herself through the rearview mirror.

"How could I be so heartless? How could I kill somebody in cold blood and don't feel a thing after it? Am I a monster? Am I heartless?" Lala asked the questions out loud as she sat in the car.

A tap on the window snapped her out of her daze. She was so far gone in her thoughts she didn't even see Lorenzo walk up to the car. When she looked over he was standing there with a smile on his face.

"You out here looking for me"? Lorenzo asked, opening her door.

"Yeah, I saw what happened on the news this morning. After you didn't come home last night, I started riding around looking for your car. I was just about to come home and start checking the hospitals," Lala lied.

She got out of the car and wrapped her arms around Lorenzo. "I was worried about you. I'm glad you're okay.

"I apologize, I should've called you. But yo, it's been crazy," Lorenzo said, as they just stood there in the driveway and talked about the events that happened last night. Lorenzo explained in detail about the fight and his trip to the hospital. He even showed her the knot on the back of his head from the bottle.

When it came to Lala explaining her night, she lied and said she fell asleep watching a movie. That sounded much better than telling him that she was up all night plotting to kill Carmen, especially since Lorenzo was going to get the call any minute now that Carmen was dead. Lala didn't want any parts of that homicide coming back to her in any way shape or form. There was no telling what Lorenzo would do if he found out that she was the culprit behind her death.

There was one thing that ate Lala up to the point where she almost blew her cover inquiring about it. She wondered if Lorenzo knew about the little girl Carmen had that looked just like him. He never mentioned having a daughter before and that was something that Lala was sure that he would have told her. Lorenzo loved kids and she couldn't imagine him not doting over his own. Lala had enough sense to know she would just have to wait until the issue washed ashore on its own.

"You're not getting nervous on me are you?" Tony asked, coming into the presidential suite he had gotten for Dior.

No, everything is perfect," Dior responded as her silhouette reflected from the glass. "This view truly is breathtaking," she said, as she stood in front of the massive window, taking in all that LA had to offer.

While Dior was taking in one view, Tony was taking in another. He couldn't peel his eyes off the forest green J. Mendel dress Dior was wearing. He wasn't sure if it was the two high slits or two dipping slashes on the upper body that had Dior giving off sex appeal in spades. Tony had no doubt that Max would be even more pleased when he met their new cast edition in person. Dior had that special something that nobody could duplicate which meant nobody could replace.

"I'll be downstairs in the lobby. The meeting with Max is in a half hour," Tony said, walking over and placing the hotel room key on the table.

"Cool, I'll be down there shortly", she responded as she continued to stare out the window as if in a trance.

Once Tony left, Dior walked over to her purse and pulled out the business card Phenomenon had given her. When she had run into him outside, she asked him for Lorenzo's phone number. She lost her iPhone in the midst of the mayhem so he wrote Lorenzo's number down for her on the back of his card. She decided now was the perfect time to call him before she went downstairs.

Seeing Lorenzo last night shattered any misconceptions Dior had that she wasn't still in love with him. On the contrary, she was very much in love and it sent a chill down her spine when he admitted that he was still in love with her too. She hadn't had the opportunity to say those words to him and he needed to know. Dior picked up her phone and dialed the number. To her disappointment it went straight to voicemail so Dior left a message.

Hi Lorenzo, it's me Dior. It was so good seeing you last night. I'm in LA right now but would love for us to link up. Please call whenever you get this message, and by the way, I'm still in love with you too. Dior left her number before hanging up. She went back to gazing out of the window, thinking to herself that she may have lost a lot but hopefully she was going to gain so much more, especially when it came to Lorenzo. She wanted her man back. Dior's road had been rough and well traveled but she wouldn't change a thing. Not in her love life or her life in general. She had moved from Philly to New York with only a dollar and a dream. Her struggle was real.

Dior had gone from boosting clothes to transporting packages of drugs to then meeting Sway and basically becoming his glorified personal whore. He got her off the streets but it came with a heavy price, so heavy that it almost ended her life. Then there was Lorenzo, who Dior considered the one true love of her life. There was also Erick, who she loved dearly but in a different way than the love she shared with Lorenzo. Both men had the biggest influence on her life though, and she didn't have any idea how the love triangle would play out.

Dior soaked up the amazing view of the city one last time before walking away from the window. The life she once had was behind her. It was now new beginnings, ones that consisted of a promising career and limitless success. It was at this very moment Dior knew that her legacy started now. She was going to make sure she did everything in her power to leave a lasting mark in

Hollywood, the city where dreams are either made or broken.

Stay Tuned For More Dior...

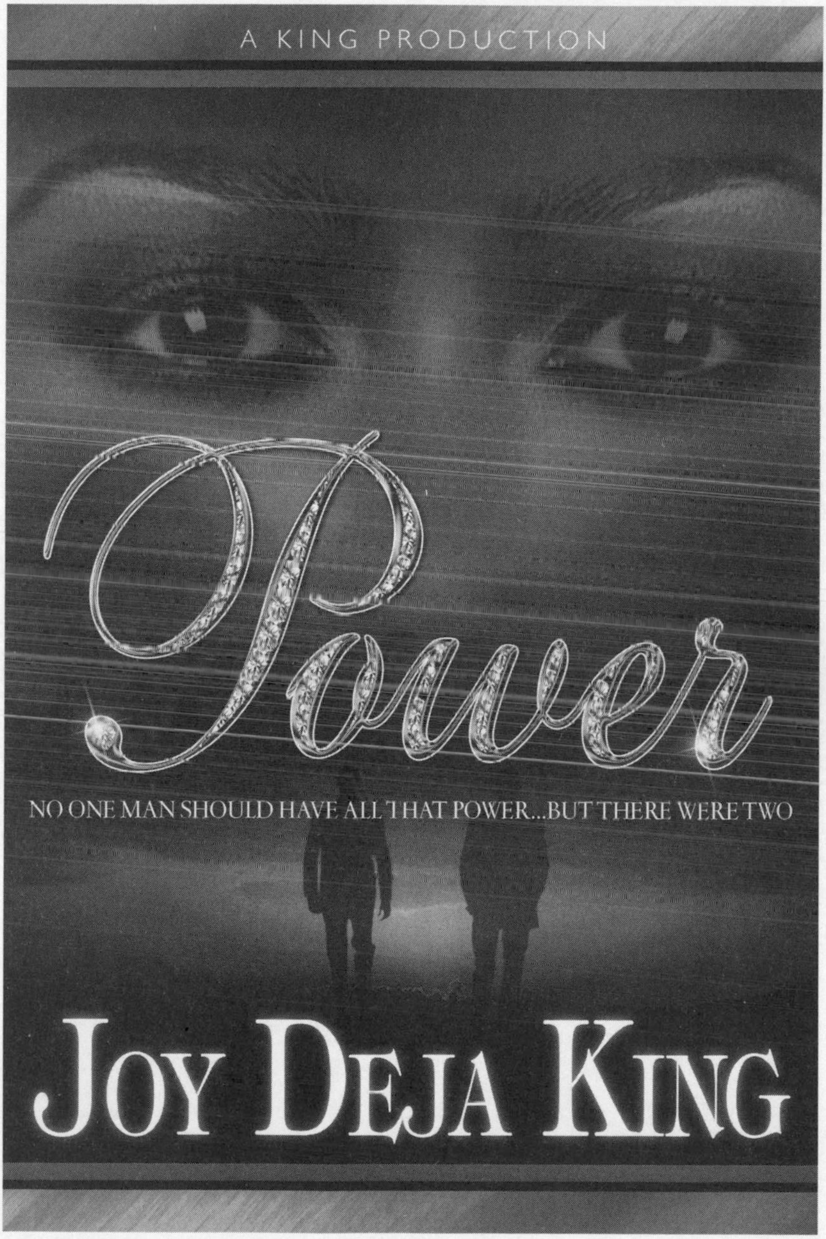
A KING PRODUCTION
Power
NO ONE MAN SHOULD HAVE ALL THAT POWER...BUT THERE WERE TWO
JOY DEJA KING

Chapter 1

Underground King

Alex stepped into his attorney's office to discuss what was always his number one priority…business. When he sat down their eyes locked and there was complete silence for the first few seconds. This was Alex's way of setting the tone of the meeting. His silence spoke volumes. This might've been his attorney's office but he was the head nigga in charge and nothing got started until he decided it was time to speak. Alex felt this approach was necessary. You see, after all these years of them doing business, attorney George Lofton still wasn't used to dealing with a man like Alex; a dirt-poor kid who could've easily died in the projects he was born in, but instead made millions. It wasn't done the ski mask way but it was still illegal.

They'd first met when Alex was a sixteen-year-old kid growing up in TechWood Homes, a housing project in Atlanta. Alex and his best friend, Deion, had been arrested because the principal found 32 crack vials in Alex's book bag. Another kid had tipped the principal off and the principal subsequently called the police. Alex and Deion were arrested and suspended from school. His mother called George, who had the charges against them dismissed and they were allowed to go back to school. But that wasn't the last time he would use George. He was arrested at twenty-two for attempted murder and for trafficking cocaine a year later. Alex was acquitted on both charges. George Lofton later became known as the best trial attorney in Atlanta, but Alex had also become the best at what he did. And since it was Alex's money that kept Mr. Lofton in designer suits, million dollar homes and foreign cars, he believed he called the shots, and dared his attorney to tell him differently.

Alex noticed that what seemed like a long period of silence made Mr. Lofton feel uncomfortable, which he liked. Out of habit, in order to camouflage the discomfort, his attorney always kept bottled water within arm's reach. He would cough then take a swig, lean back in his chair, raise his eyebrows a little, trying to give a look of certainty, though he wasn't completely confident at all in Alex's presence. The reason was because Alex did what many had thought would be impossible, especially men like George Lofton. He had gone from a knucklehead, low-level drug dealer to an underground king and an unstoppable respected criminal boss.

Before finally speaking, Alex gave an intense stare into George Lofton's piercing eyes. They were not only the bluest he had ever seen, but also some of the most calculating. The latter is what Alex found so compelling. A calculating attorney working on his behalf could almost guarantee a get out of jail card for the duration of his criminal career.

"Have you thought over what we briefly discussed the other day?" Alex asked his attorney, finally breaking the silence.

"Yes I have, but I want to make sure I understand you correctly. You want to give me six hundred thousand to represent you or your friend Deion if you are ever arrested and have to stand trial again in the future?"

Alex assumed he had already made himself clear based on their previous conversations and was annoyed by what he now considered a repetitive question. "George, you know I don't like repeating myself. That's exactly what I'm saying. Are we clear?"

"So this is an unofficial retainer."

"Yes, you can call it that."

George stood and closed the blinds then walked over to the door that led to the reception area. He turned the deadbolt so they wouldn't be disturbed. George sat back behind the desk. "You know that if you and your friend Deion are ever on the same case that I can't represent the both of you."

"I know that."

"So what do you propose I do if that was ever to happen?"

"You would get him the next best attorney in

Atlanta," Alex said without hesitation. Deion was Alex's best friend—had been since the first grade. They were now business partners, but the core of their bond was built on that friendship, and because of that Alex would always look out for Deion's best interest.

"That's all I need to know."

Alex clasped his hands and stared at the ceiling for a moment thinking that maybe it was a bad idea bringing the money to George. Maybe he should have just put it somewhere safe only known to him and his mom. He quickly dismissed his concerns.

"Okay. Where's the money?" Alex presented him with two leather briefcases. George opened the first one and was glad to see that it was all hundred-dollar bills. When he closed the briefcase he asked, "There is no need to count this is there?"

"You can count it if you want, but it's all there."

George took another swig of water. The cash made him nervous. He planned to take it directly to one of his bank safe deposit boxes. The two men stood. Alex was a foot taller than George; he had flawless mahogany skin, a deep brown with a bit of a red tint, broad shoulders, very large hands, and a goatee. He was a man's man. With such a powerful physical appearance, Alex kept his style very low-key. His only display of wealth was a pricey diamond watch that his best friend and partner Deion had bought him for his birthday.

"I'll take good care of this, and you," his attorney

said, extending his hand to Alex.

"With this type of money, I know you will," Alex stated without flinching. Alex gave one last lingering stare into his attorney's piercing eyes. "We do have a clear understanding…correct?"

"Of course. I've never let you down and I never will. That, I promise you." The men shook hands and Alex made his exit with the same coolness as his entrance.

With Alex embarking on a new, potentially dangerous business venture, he wanted to make sure that he had all his bases covered. The higher up he seemed to go on the totem pole, the costlier his problems became. But Alex welcomed new challenges because he had no intentions of ever being a nickel and dime nigga again.

A KING PRODUCTION
Still The Baddest Bitch
A Novel
JOY DEJA KING

A KING PRODUCTION
Baller
Bitches
VOLUME 2
PARTS 4-6
A NOVEL
JOY DEJA KING